samurai girl
The Book of the Flame

samurai girl

samurai girl

The Book of the Flame

Carrie Asai

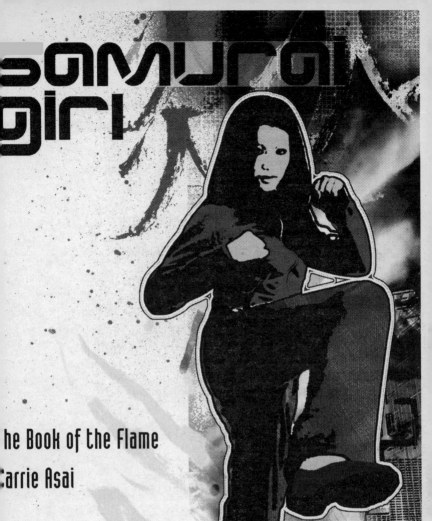

SIMON AND SCHUSTER

SIMON AND SCHUSTER

First published in Great Britain in 2005 by Simon & Schuster UK Ltd,
A Viacom Company
Africa House, 64-78 Kingsway, London WC2B 6AH

Originally published in 2004 by Simon Pulse an imprint
of Simon & Schuster Children's Division. New York

 Produced by 17th Street Productions.
An Alloy Company.
151 West 26th Street, New York, NY 10011

Text copyright © 2004 by 17th Street Productions, an Alloy company.
Cover illustration copyright © 2004 Chenna@www.synergyart.co.uk

A CIP catalogue record for this book is
available from the British Library

ISBN 0 689 86131 1

1 3 5 7 9 10 8 6 4 2

Printed and bound in Great Britain by Cox & Wyman, Reading, Berkshire

Tokyo
Daily
News

February 26, 2004

At 12:03 A.M. last night, per police logs, a burglary was reported by staff at the exclusive Kazashi Clinic in Mizuho. Go Watanebe, the clinic's director, declined comment, but an anonymous source told the *Daily News* that around 11 P.M., a nurse discovered that the clinic's drug supplies had been plundered. "They knew what they were doing," the source said, "because they took a bunch of morphine and Valium and other drugs with a high street-market value." Police refused to answer questions about a possible link between the drug theft and Konishi Kogo (currently the clinic's most well known patient), who was flown back to Japan two months ago after an attack by an unknown assailant in Los Angeles. Okichi Ono, head nurse at the clinic, stated that Kogo is in stable condition but remains comatose. Kogo's adopted daughter, Heaven Kogo, has been missing since her wedding day four months ago, when a masked intruder (some sources have said a ninja) disrupted the ceremony and murdered her brother, Ohiko Kogo.

Las Vegas Sun

February 28, 2004

Police are searching for a man who they believe may have information about Heaven Kogo, a Japanese national currently on the California State Police's missing persons list. The man was recently seen in several Strip locales, including the Hard Rock Hotel and Mandalay Bay, in the company of a woman fitting the description of Heaven Kogo. Sources describe the man as a "high roller" who frequents VIP rooms at casinos and clubs on the Strip and who sometimes travels with an entourage. Anyone with information about the above individual is asked to call 1-800-TIPS4US.

1

"Shut up. And tell your boyfriend to shut up, too," Pablo snapped.

I clamped my mouth shut and looked over at Hiro, who sat next to me in the backseat of the black sedan. An ugly-looking bruise was spreading across Hiro's left cheek (those beautiful cheekbones!) and blood trickled down his forehead. His lower lip was swollen, and his jeans were covered in dirt and more blood. And if the pain that racked my body was any sign, I didn't look much better myself. We'd just crossed the Mexican border into California (thanks to the handful of cash I'd seen Pablo cram into the customs officer's pocket), and I had no idea where we were headed.

Hiro shook his head at me slowly.

"Do what he says," he mouthed, and I nodded, trying to stop the swell of tears I felt stinging my eyes. It was unbearable to think that I might be leading Hiro to his death. This was my fight, my battle, and these thugs, whoever they were, wanted me, not him. Now, for the first time since my long journey had begun, I couldn't see a way out. We were going almost a hundred miles an hour through the California desert. My hands were tightly bound behind my back, with a rope connecting them to my ankles, which were also bound. I felt like a cow being led to the slaughter, helpless and doomed.

I was propped up awkwardly against Hiro, unable to sit up straight. After a few minutes I felt him writhing against me. "Are you hurt?" I whispered. Hiro shook his head but kept squirming. I looked nervously toward the front seat, where Pablo sat puffing a huge cigar and driving way too fast. It was hard to believe that when Teddy had introduced me to Pablo back in Vegas, I hadn't immediately sensed what a dangerous guy he was—as if the blingy jewelry and greased-back hair weren't enough, he had a mouthful of gold teeth. I prayed he and his cohort wouldn't turn around.

I glanced back at Hiro. The veins on his neck stuck out from the effort he was making not to move as he worked at the cord around his wrists. I held my breath right along with him, willing Pablo and Co. not to look. I wasn't sure if "escape artist" was on Hiro's list of abilities, but I hoped so.

Hiro gave a tight-lipped smile. I looked down. The ropes holding him had gone slack. He'd wriggled his way out.

My heart leapt. Maybe this wasn't the end. Hiro

motioned with his eyes that I should maneuver into a position where he could work on the knots that bound me without being seen. I scooted around in the seat, focused all the time on Pablo and his buddy, who both seemed to be intent on celebrating with their nasty-smelling cigars. In between puffs they growled at each other in Spanish, and the unknown thug, who had a bristling mustache that couldn't hide the ugly scar slashing across his lip and down his jawline, kept gesturing with his gun for emphasis.

In a few moments I was free. I resisted the urge to stretch my arms and legs—or to hurl myself into Hiro's arms, to hug him and tell him I was sorry for this, for all of this. As if in answer to my thoughts, the car jolted without warning, throwing Hiro against me.

"Your mission is to achieve heightened perception," he whispered in my ear. "You must be aware of everything around you. That's the only way you're going to make it."

"What's going on back there? Didn't I tell you to shut up?" Mustache (as I'd come to think of him) turned around and waved his gun at us. My heart pounded as I cringed back against the seat. Having a gun shoved in your face in real life is freaking scary. Any bravery you might have on top just oozes right out of you. And I was terrified he'd notice that we were no longer tied up.

"I just wanted to make sure she was okay," Hiro said, his voice calm.

"You can't help your little girlfriend anymore," Mustache

leered, his grin twisted and grotesque. "Just do as you're told."

He turned around, and Hiro gave me a look that said, "Simmer down." I stared out the window into the glaring heat.

I had a lot of work to do. First I had to pull myself out of my body to try to forget about the pain and stiffness that always set in after a fight. Then I had to clear my head of the images—the gang of mystery men bursting into our hotel room, the thud and thunk of the bone-crushing kicks and punches, the sight of Teddy sliding down to the ground, his back covered in blood. . . .

I squeezed my eyes shut, as if that could help drive the images away. I'd seen Teddy slump to the floor, bloody and broken, and when Pablo and his gang finally had beaten us into submission and dragged us from the motel room, I'd noticed smears of blood on the low wall by the open window. Whether Teddy had jumped or been thrown, I didn't know. But he had died alone. I'd looked for his body on our way out of the building, but it was already gone, probably dragged off by one of Pablo's henchmen.

There was no question in my mind that I was responsible. When I'd run into Teddy in Vegas, I'd been so happy to see someone I felt was on my side, who really *knew* my story, that I'd overlooked the dangers of us being seen together. Even though I believed his family, the Yukemuras (who were yakuza—Japanese mafia, just like mine, as I'd recently discovered), were still after me, and even though I knew that Teddy was involved with Colombian drug runners . . . Not exactly the most savory set of circumstances.

I'd tried not to think about it. But I'd agreed to flee Vegas with him because I thought Hiro had abandoned me. I'd used Teddy. He was no innocent, but his heart was certainly in the right place. And now he was gone. Just like that. I felt like such a stupid idiot. What had I planned to tell him when the three of us eventually made it to Europe, like we'd planned? *"Thanks a bunch, Teddy! I know you loved me and saved my life, but I want to be with Hiro now! See ya!"* Stupid.

I tried to untangle the thoughts teeming in my head, but it seemed like as soon as I put one to rest, another jumped to fill its place—and my brain just kept digging deeper. The first images that floated to the surface were of my father, lying in a coma in Japan, and my dead brother, Ohiko—I was still no closer to finding out who wanted my family dead. I imagined my father lying in a crisp white hospital bed, my stepmother, Mieko, at his side. Then I wondered again about her involvement in all that had happened, and my mind lingered on the confrontation I'd had with Marcus and his gangbangers on a subway platform in L.A. *"Your step-mother says hello,"* he'd said.

I squeezed my eyes tightly shut and let my mind drift past that memory and on to the next. Cheryl, my only friend in L.A., popped up, pink-streaked hair and all. For all I knew,

7

she was dead now, too, trapped in a fire that had been set for me. I'd hurt all the people who'd tried to help me, I realized. It hurt too much to think about. . . . I pushed the images away and let a picture of Hiro take their place. I thought of the moment I found out he felt the same way about me as I did about him—and how, in order to admit it, he'd had to break Karen's heart.

Guilt, fear, shame, love, pain—so many feelings clogging up the works. I tried every technique in the book, first visualizing bundling up my thoughts into a neat package and hurling them out the car window into the dusty desert, then imagining each one floating up out of the top of my head, leaving my mind a clean, empty slate. After what felt like forever, I managed to clear a tiny corner of my head. *Think, Heaven, think,* I told myself. *What exists around you? What can you feel? Who are the people holding you prisoner? Is there anything in the car you can use as a weapon? And most important, how can you and Hiro get yourselves out of this?*

A gentle tap on my ankle brought me back to reality. Hiro gave me a meaningful look and nodded slightly out the rear window. A silver SUV was behind us. I watched the SUV follow our sedan into a passing lane, then move smoothly back behind us when we switched lanes again.

We were being followed. I looked at Hiro and raised my eyebrows. So much for my powers of perception—I hadn't even noticed.

"We're being followed," Hiro said in a loud, clear voice.

Mustache turned around, and the SUV simultaneously slipped back into the stream of traffic, hiding itself. "Don't be a smartass," Mustache rumbled.

"Look for yourself," Hiro said steadily.

Mustache flipped around in his seat and I heard the click of his knife opening before I saw the flash of metal held to Hiro's throat. I gasped. Hiro stared silently at Mustache without moving. I started to tremble and readied myself to intervene if Mustache went too far. Was he for real? Or was he just trying to scare us?

"Que estas haciendo? Nos son inútiles si son muertos," Pablo barked. Mustache looked irritated, but he clicked his knife shut and turned around.

"You're right," he said in his thickly accented English. "They're not worth anything dead. That comes later." I couldn't see his face, but something told me he was smiling.

I caught my breath and concentrated on the SUV that was so clearly tailing us. If the thugs in the front seat were sent by the Yukemuras, as I'd thought when they first busted into the hotel room with Teddy in tow, then who the hell was following us? I watched Mustache stare into the rear- and side-view mirrors; then he and Pablo started arguing again. Suddenly Mustache flipped around and grabbed my ponytail, yanking my head back.

"Who are they?" he yelled, his funky, stinking breath

washing over my face. I shrank back against the hot leather seat, less to get away from the smell (although believe me, I wanted to) than to keep my hands and ankles hidden. I saw Hiro's face grow tight. I knew he'd lash out if he could, but he couldn't risk giving us away—our freedom was our one advantage, however small. I took a deep breath and tried to resist the pain and the urge to kick Mustache's butt.

"I don't know," I yelped, trying to sound deferential and clueless. "I really don't!" Actually, it wasn't hard—even though I wasn't the best actress, I really hadn't the slightest clue where all this was headed. But I knew it was nowhere good.

The car lurched, and Mustache lost his hold on my hair. I took the opportunity to slink out from under his grip.

"Shit!" yelled Mustache, dropping heavily back into the front seat.

"Are they better than these guys or worse?" I asked Hiro in Japanese.

"Callate!" Mustache roared. "How many times do I have to tell you to keep your mouths shut?" The engine groaned as Pablo floored the gas. Hiro and I were thrown back against our seats—full-on chase mode. The silver SUV had given up any attempt to hide itself, and soon it clung within inches of the sedan, tailgating us so close that eventually its front bumper was tapping against our back one. The sedan shuddered, and I went rigid.

"Kangaete miru na," Hiro said. "Don't think about it.

Just concentrate on what you see. Stay alert." He grabbed my hand and squeezed. I held my breath as we weaved in and out of lanes, trying to lose the SUV. Green highway signs flipped by, and in just minutes we were on the outskirts of San Diego. My heart leapt into my throat as we veered into another lane, and a red Volkswagen Bug slammed on its horn and its brakes in an attempt to avoid us. We slipped by untouched, but the Bug wasn't so lucky. A horrifying screech split the air, followed by the sound of metal crunching metal, and when I looked back, the Bug was lying on its side, sliding down the highway. Cars slowed behind the accident, but the SUV shot through like a silver dart. I almost covered my eyes before I remembered that my hands were supposedly tied.

With a sudden wrench the sedan flew across four lanes in a flurry of honking, and we careened onto an exit ramp, kicking up a stream of orange utility cones in our wake. I screamed as we blew through a stoplight at the bottom of the ramp, narrowly missing a white convertible and leaving another fender-bender pileup behind us. Two teenagers in baggy pants jumped out of the way as we squealed around a corner, and we narrowly avoided crashing into a long median planted with palm trees. I was in the grip of a fear I had never known—death was staring us in the face, and there was nothing we could do about it. Our fate was out of our hands, which was so much worse than just being in a fight—at least then you could fight back. I looked down and saw that I had dug my nails into Hiro's hand, leaving vivid red crescents on his tan skin. Was this how we were going to go? I prayed we wouldn't take any innocent pedestrians down with us.

With a sickening lurch the sedan hopped a curb and spun out onto a faded green lawn. Within seconds Pablo had whirled the car around and bashed into the SUV, which was trying to block us in on the dead-end street.

"Pendejo!" Pablo yelled, twisting the steering wheel around as far as it would go. We screeched by the SUV and turned right.

A one-way street. And we were going the wrong way.

"Put on your seat belt!" I yelled to Hiro over the wind whistling in through the open windows and the approaching sounds of sirens. It was certainly *not* the time to worry about Mustache and friend finding out we were no longer tied. Horns blared as car after car came right at us before veering aside—the world's deadliest game of chicken. I snapped my seat belt in place and looked at Hiro for the last time. We were doing eighty on a residential street. Hiro stared into my eyes.

"I love you, Heaven Kogo," he said.

I grabbed his hand. "Yes," I answered, then looked away. I don't know why I said it, why I ignored the voice in my head that chanted, *I love you too, I love you, I love you.* The words wouldn't come. I was filled with a deep sadness at the prospect of our deaths. I felt an overwhelming tenderness for Hiro, for myself, for *life*. A red light loomed ahead. We weren't slowing down. As we crossed the inter-section, I saw a car heading straight for us.

And then the car hit.

2

It's true—your life really does flash before your eyes. The scream of tires ripped through the air just before the sonic boom of an impact so strong, it felt like my bones were trying to escape from my body. I screamed and braced myself against the seat, and my head crashed against the window as another blow rocked our spinning sedan. And then . . .

Time stopped—the crunch and wail of two huge machines hitting each other at high speed, Hiro's warm body next to me, the thugs up front, my own body strapped into the car, the heat and dust . . . it all vanished in a wash of red and orange, and I was suddenly out of time, trapped in some weird, floating tableau of my life, tumbling through scene after scene. The odd thing was that I was seeing some events that I couldn't actually remember but that I knew had happened: my real mother, who I'd never known, boarding the ill-fated JAL flight to Los Angeles all those years ago . . . me again, only six months old, lying in a heap of wreckage, the only survivor of the downed plane . . . my father, Konishi, screaming at my brother, Ohiko, just before he left the compound forever . . . the night my father told me I was going to marry Teddy Yukemura. The images came faster now, speeding up. . . . Ohiko's death at the hands of the ninja whose attack had stopped the wedding . . . my escape on foot into the dark L.A. night . . . finding Hiro and, later, him agreeing to train me . . . the first time he kissed me. . . .

Another mind-jarring thud and it was over. My head whipped backward and I was suddenly back in my own body, sick with the smell of gasoline and burnt rubber. I shook my head to clear away the haze. We had crunched to a stop.

"Are you okay?" I gasped, grabbing Hiro's shoulder.

"Fine, fine. But you're bleeding." He wiped blood off my forehead.

"I hit my head on the window," I said. For some reason I felt totally calm, as though the crash had happened in a dream from which I still hadn't woken up.

"You sure did," Hiro said, a look of concern flitting over his face. I followed his glance to the window on my side of the car—it was cracked from where my head had bashed it. "Come on, we've got to get out of here." Hiro snapped open my seat belt.

"My door's stuck," I yelled. Mustache was collapsed in

the twisted front seat, which was awash in blood. Pablo had gone through the windshield. One of his hands, the thick gold rings coated in gore, lay awkwardly on the dashboard next to his hip, nestled in a pile of broken glass. Something told me the hand wasn't attached to his arm anymore. My stomach churned and I tore my eyes away. I didn't want to get any closer to them than I had to. Hiro stretched out on the seat and kicked against his door. Nothing. I heard a whoosh, and the acrid smell of burning gasoline filled the air. Black smoke poured into the car through the destroyed windshield, oozing around Pablo's body as if he had just bent over to take a quick peek into the fires of hell.

The engine was on fire. "Hurry!" I screamed, still struggling with my own door. I coughed as the smoke slipped up my nose.

Hiro smashed against the door again, but it wouldn't budge. "Give me your sweatshirt."

I shucked it off, and Hiro rolled it around his fist. "Turn around." I hid my face, taking the opportunity to rub my stinging eyes. Hiro punched through the window and tore out the leftover pieces of glass. He dragged me toward him and I scrambled through, ignoring the pinch of the remaining shards as they shredded the knees of my jeans. Hiro was right behind me, and we both dropped onto the pavement and stumbled away from the smoking wreck. A crowd had started to gather.

"Keep away from the car!" Hiro shouted. "It's going to blow!"

A communal gasp went up and the crowd stepped back toward the other side of the street. I heard the sirens coming closer and looked around for the SUV. It lay on its side about forty feet away. The door popped open and two men tumbled out of the wreck. I blinked, not quite sure I was seeing what I thought I was—yes, it was them, all right. The same Yukemura henchmen who had been after me since the kidnapping-that-wasn't.

"They're Yukemura men!" I grabbed Hiro's arm. "So who the hell were *those* guys?" I gestured at the black sedan.

"We'll figure it out later—we've got to get out of here."

A blond woman pushed out of the crowd and ran toward us. "I'm a doctor. You need to sit down until the ambulance gets here."

"We're fine," Hiro said, "but those guys are pretty banged up." The doctor looked skeptical. "Sit down here and don't move," she commanded, and then ran over to the Yukemura men, who tried to push past her. They started to argue.

"What about Mustache?" I asked Hiro. "And Pablo?" I added with a shiver, picturing his disembodied hand again.

Hiro's face tightened. "I think they're gone."

No sooner had the words left his mouth than an enormous, earth-shattering explosion ripped through the air— the sedan's gas tank had finally blown. The crowd ducked in unison and people started screaming. A fire truck roared around the corner as three police cruisers screeched to the scene, adding to the madness. Thick black smoke billowed up into the sky.

"Run. Now." Hiro grabbed my hand and we bolted, flying across the intersection and into an alley. I heard what I presumed were police officers calling for us to stop, but I knew that if we got caught, we wouldn't have a prayer of figuring out what was going on. And for all I knew, our Yukemura-clan friends from the SUV would kill us on the spot if they found us.

"Dead end," I gasped as we approached a chain-link fence. Hiro rattled it in frustration.

"Dammit!" he shouted. I looked wildly around for another way out. A shabby door to our right looked promising, but it wouldn't give when I tried it. I barreled against it, trying to use my shoulder to bust through. No dice. And it hurt like hell.

"You're just going to hurt yourself," Hiro said, seeing me grimace. "Come on—we have to go over." I ran to the fence and started climbing, Hiro right behind me. We launched ourselves over the top just as the policemen spun into the alley.

"There they are!"

We sprinted down the alley and out into the maze of San Diego. I'd never been here, and I had no idea if Hiro had either—there was no time to ask. The city was a blur as we flew down the residential streets. I remembered again the night I'd escaped from my own wedding. It had been Halloween then—not even six months had passed, but since that night I'd lived enough for a whole lifetime.

This time is different, I told myself. *You have Hiro now, and it's day, not night.* But it was cold comfort. I felt like the intervening months had slipped away and I was right back where I'd started—still running for safety. Was I any better off than I had been back then? I still had no idea who'd killed my brother, and I'd managed to leave a trail of broken lives in my path as I searched for the answer. *But at least you're not the same girl you were then,* droned a voice in my head.

It was true. No matter what, I'd never go back to being the scared, spoiled, clueless little girl I'd been when I arrived in L.A. for the wedding. I was Samurai Girl now—even if I still managed to screw up on a regular basis.

"Hiro!" I breathed as a cramp ripped through my side. "I'm cramping." I slowed to a trot. "Please—we've been running forever."

Hiro slowed down, sweat dripping from his forehead. "I know, but it's not safe here."

"Where is?" I gasped, suddenly filled with despair. "We don't know anyone here. *Look* at us—no matter how far we run, people are still going to be suspicious. Hell, *I'd* call the cops if I saw you sprinting past me! We need to get cleaned up."

Hiro stopped, breathing hard, and looked me up and

down. "You're right," he said, bending over to stretch. "We're not going to get very far looking like this."

"Thank you," I said, overjoyed that we'd actually stopped moving. I wanted to hurl myself onto the nearest lawn, where a sprinkler was tick-ticking a delicious spray out over the green, green grass. It was early afternoon, and the day had grown terribly hot. I stepped closer to the sprinkler, hoping to catch a few stray drops. "We need to go to a gas station or something. If we try to check into a motel, we'll get busted for sure."

Hiro nodded. "Okay. Let's find someplace to clean up, and then we can figure out our next move."

I hobbled after Hiro as he strode down the block. No matter how much he fought or how much energy he exerted, he always seemed to have just a little extra reserve from which to draw. He was a machine. I, on the other hand, felt like I had been run over by a truck.

"Go around to the side. I'll follow with the keys. I don't want to draw more suspicion than we have to." I ducked around the side of the squat convenience store building as Hiro went in. After a few minutes he came out carrying a shopping bag.

"Please tell me you bought some water," I said.

Hiro pulled a bottle of water from the bag, and I gulped it so fast, it ran down my chin and neck. Hiro chugged from his own bottle. When I finally came up for air, Hiro took the bottle back.

"That's enough for now. You'll make yourself sick." Hiro pulled some stuff out of the bag, then handed it to me. "Here—go clean up. I'll be next door."

I went into the ladies' bathroom, relieved to find that it wasn't quite as disgusting as I'd expected. Someone had even tried to cheer up the dank little cell by posting a picture of some kittens frolicking in a flower patch on one of the grayish walls. Cute. I opened the bag and took out a bar of soap, a package of those synthetic towels like you wash your dishes or windshield with, a comb, and a black tank top that said SAN DIEGO on it in garish pink neon letters. I gingerly peeled off my filthy T-shirt. The mirror was merciless.

I was *covered* in bruises. The ones from the fight back in Tijuana had blossomed into an ominous purple-black shade, while the fresh ones from the crash were still that faded blue color. The worst was the combination bruise–fabric burn that tore across my collarbone and all the way down my chest—a perfect impression of the seat belt. It throbbed, but it was a small price to pay—I could have ended up like Pablo.

I willed the image out of my head. *Think kittens,* I told myself, staring at the poster. *So cute, cuddly, and healthy . . .*

With my remaining elastic I piled my hair on top of my head, wet one of the cloths, and soaped myself as gently as I could. At least my face didn't look too bad. I was ready to get to work on my hair, which was caked with blood and

21

muck, when I heard a soft knock at the door. I pulled the tank top on.

"Who is it?"

"It's me."

I opened the door and Hiro slid inside.

"Did anyone see you?" I whispered.

"I don't think so." A smile flitted across Hiro's now clean but still battered face. Even the swelling couldn't hide his good looks. My heart melted a little just looking at him. *Way to be serious about the situation,* I told myself. *How about giving your hormones a rest for a minute or three?*

"What?" I asked, feeling self-conscious.

"Nice shirt."

I rolled my eyes. "Well, *you* picked it out." I plucked at the fabric. "It's a little tight. What size is it?"

"Small."

"Hiro! I'm five-nine! And—thanks to you—on my way to muscle-bound. Small is for tiny girls!"

"You would look beautiful in a paper bag, Heaven," Hiro said, his voice softening. "It looks hot." He put his arms around my waist and pulled me gently toward him. Our lips met, and Hiro flinched.

"What is it?" I pulled back, looking into his black eyes.

"Sorry—it stings." I gently ran my fingers over Hiro's swollen lip, then kissed him as lightly as I could. He warmed to the kiss and soon we were engaged in full lip lock. The bathroom disappeared and I was far away.

Too soon, Hiro broke the kiss. I gulped, resting my head on his shoulder. The kittens stared back at me from the wall, and I winked at them, just because I wanted to. I still felt shy about our romantic interactions. After all, I wasn't exactly experienced. In fact, I was totally, completely *in*experienced.

"We'd better get going. But the question is, where?" Hiro's voice assumed a businesslike tone. The moment had passed. I untangled myself from his arms and leaned back against the sink. I'd been contemplating just that question while I was tending to my battered body.

"I can't run anymore, Hiro." I sighed.

"What does that mean, exactly?" Hiro asked, looking concerned.

"It means I'm not getting anywhere with all this . . . this *mystery*. It seems pretty clear at this point that there's more than one group of people after us—there was Marcus and his gang of thugs. And you know that had something to do with Mieko. . . ."

"We don't know what your stepmother's role in this whole thing is yet," Hiro said, crossing his arms. "And it doesn't change the fact that most signs point to the Yukemuras."

"Exactly," I agreed, "we have no idea. But don't you see that's why I—we—have to stop running? We need to look for the answers ourselves, not wait for them to come to us. And that's why I want to go back to L.A. and talk to Yoji Yukemura."

23

"Are you serious?" Hiro asked skeptically.

"Totally. Look—you said it before: It always comes back to the Yukemuras. Even those guys who kidnapped us back in Tijuana had something to do with Teddy, and do we really know how deep Teddy's drug deals went? Maybe he was still into some of his father's yakuza stuff."

"Well, you'd know more than I. . . ."

Was that jealousy I heard in Hiro's voice? He'd been none too happy about having Teddy around and even less psyched when he realized that I'd agreed to marry him. Of course, that had been before Hiro finally showed up (late) and everything became clear. I'd explained to Hiro that the engagement had just been part of my plan to get out of Vegas, and I was almost positive he believed me. But that didn't stop him from being irritated.

"Unfortunately, I don't," I snapped. "It's not like we spent that much time chatting." It seemed ridiculous to be talking about this right now—especially since Teddy was dead.

Hiro raised his eyebrows. "That's not what I mean and you know it."

This was a side of Hiro I'd never suspected existed. I blundered on. "Teddy's father has got to have some answers. And if I know what he knows, then maybe I can end this thing for good." I rubbed my eyes. "We just can't go on like this."

"Heaven," Hiro said, his voice softening. "Do you

really think Yoji's going to be in a good mood when he hears that his son is dead and you were there when it happened? He's going to be furious. Who knows what he might do?"

"He needs me alive," I said. *That* I was sure about. "He always has. Yoji needs the Kogo money to fix his business. It's crumbling. You know that's why the wedding was arranged in the first place and why Teddy tried so hard to get to me after I ran away. If he kills me—boom!" I slapped my hands together for emphasis. "That's it. He's not going to see a penny of it. But if he wants answers about what happened to Teddy, then I can help him. *We* can help him get the revenge he wants."

Hiro ran his hand through his hair, and for a moment all I could hear was the drip of a leaky pipe and the distant sound of traffic from the street. I knew I was making the right decision. I prayed that Hiro would understand. "Revenge is not the samurai way," Hiro finally said. "Justice, yes. But Teddy's death isn't ours to avenge."

"Oh, come *on*, Hiro," I pleaded. "We've broken just about every tenet of the bushido so far. I mean, you and me—we're *together*. And you're my sensei."

"I know we haven't exactly adhered to the samurai code," Hiro said, "but these circumstances are unique. That doesn't mean we can just throw everything we strive for out the window. If we do, then we're just rogue samurai—ronin. Warriors for hire."

25

"I'm not proposing that we hire ourselves out to Yoji to avenge Teddy's death," I insisted. "I'm just saying we have some information that Yoji wants. Besides, what else can we do?"

Hiro was silent. Fatigue washed over me, and my legs started trembling. I flipped the toilet cover down and sat on it. I hated myself for being able to talk so matter-of-factly about Teddy's death, as if it were nothing more than one false move in a dangerous game we'd been playing. What was *happening* to me? Was this part of becoming a warrior? Or were the last bits of my compassion and humanity slipping away? I'd cared for Teddy—not in the way I cared about Hiro, but as a friend, and a close one at that. Teddy was a troubled soul, but he was *good* deep down, a sweetheart. In private, he was gentle. And he'd loved me.

"Okay, Heaven," Hiro said, pulling me gently to my feet. "You're right. We need to confront Yoji. I just want you to be safe."

"I know you do," I said, relieved, and put my arms around him. "Trust me."

Hiro tipped my face back and kissed me gently. "I do." We embraced again, then he stepped away. "So, back to L.A.?" he asked.

"Yep. What do you think? The bus?"

Hiro shook his head. "Too risky. They'll be staking out the bus and train stations. We'd better rent a car." He paused. "So what happens when we get there? How are we going to find Yoji?"

"I've got a plan," I answered, smiling.

"Uh-oh," Hiro joked. "I remember what happened the last time you said that."

"Ha ha," I said, and tapped him lightly on the arm. "Come on—I've got to do something about this hair." I looked in the mirror and sighed. The thought of getting all the gunk and tangles out of my hair with nothing but a bar of soap and a fifty-cent comb depressed me to no end.

"Let me help. Here, sit down."

I bent my head over the sink as Hiro lathered the soap into my hair.

"I think that's the best we can do," he said after a few minutes. He patted my mane down with one of the handi cloths, but more brown water just dripped out of it. I felt like a drowned dog.

"I'm never going to get this untangled." My eyes met Hiro's in the mirror. "Should we cut it?" I asked impulsively.

"It would probably be best, but . . ." Hiro's voice trailed off, and he put his arm around my shoulders.

"Do it," I said, with more authority than I actually felt. "Besides—the added bonus is that it will make me look different. We can go undercover." I scanned Hiro's serious face. "Maybe we should do something about yours, too."

Hiro ran his hands through his hair again. "Dye?"

27

SAMURAI GIRL

"I always wondered what you'd look like as a bottle blond," I joked softly.

Hiro nodded. "I'll go get the stuff."

I sat down and waited for Hiro to return. I knew I was making the right decisions. But sometimes the right decisions hurt.

28

We do my hair first so that the bleach can set while I'm cutting Heaven's. She is silent as the first dark strands fall to the ground. I can't help thinking that I should be able to protect her from this sort of thing, that if I were a better man, she wouldn't have to go to such lengths to be free of the evil that follows her. But at the same time—she's grown so much! The Heaven who showed up on my doorstep in her wedding dress, shivering and covered in blood, would never have let me cut her hair. She was so young then, still trapped by the lavish lifestyle she'd led with her adoptive family. Now she is fierce—a strong, capable woman.

"How's it going?" she says, her eyes searching for mine in the mirror.

"I think I'm getting the hang of it," I tell her, wanting to throw the scissors down and hug her, comfort her, press her body to mine.

"Let's do a sort of geisha thing—some bangs, a bob. Very hip." She grins, and my heart melts. Having her in my life makes everything lighter. And it makes me stronger. I snip away at the dark locks.

I've known for a while now that she and I were meant to be together, and every passing minute only solidifies that decision for me. She has a deep kindness inside her—and she is a talented warrior. Her goal right now is clear—but what is mine? To help her untangle this mystery—but then what? Will we be able to build a life for ourselves? An honest life? Will she still want me after this is over?

There is doubt, I have to admit. When she is next to me, everything is clear, but as soon as I turn away, my mind veers off on a different path and I can't help wondering what happened between her and Teddy and how it was that she allowed him to believe that she would marry him. I know she thought that I had abandoned her, but it is this impetuousness, this rashness, that bothers me. She is so quick to despair. Does her heart truly belong to me? Or is she so desperate to avenge her family, her brother, Ohiko, that she has become somewhat mercenary? When I think of her and Teddy together in Joshua Tree, I start to think all sorts of horrible things—how close were they? Where did they sleep? Is she different with him than with me?

Perhaps that is just simple jealousy. I shouldn't make too much of it. It is normal to have these feelings—the important part is not to let them poison all that is good between us. Teddy is gone now, and I should not rejoice at that. He was a simple fellow, really, just as much a victim as Heaven. They can't help it that their families became involved in such things. Any more than I could help . . .

The past is the past. But these doubts still bother me—I haven't thought so much about my own family since I left Japan so many years ago. I was young then and couldn't anticipate what was to come. Now I see all too clearly what might happen.

I snip away the last of it.

Heaven stands up and runs her fingers through what's

left of her hair. She is breathtaking.

"I love it," she says. "I know this isn't, like, a fashion moment, but you've got some real talent there, mister!"

I put the scissors down and kiss her. She is so soft, so perfect.

She pulls away and shakes her finger at me.

"Let's get that bleach out of your hair, or you're going to look like Gwen Stefani."

I lean my head over the sink.

I love her. I trust her. I will keep her safe. This is my only duty now.

Hiko

3

"Take a right up here," I told Hiro. He turned off West Sunset and headed deeper into Chinatown. The warm wind blew in through the windows of the car and ruffled what was left of my hair. I checked myself out for the millionth time in the side mirror, still not quite believing how different I looked—for a haircut done by an amateur in a convenience store bathroom, it was pretty damn good. I looked like I had stepped out of my regular-girl lifestyle and into *The Matrix* or something. The clumsy scissors Hiro had used lent the whole 'do a kind of choppy aspect—he'd cut my bangs very short so the hair wouldn't get in my eyes, and the rest of it fell to just below my chin. I looked more badass than I ever had—but what was more important, I *felt* stronger.

Part of it had to do with getting some sleep on the drive

from San Diego. "Are you okay?" I asked Hiro, feeling guilty when I remembered that he hadn't had the benefit of a nap. I couldn't drive—had never had anywhere to drive *to* before coming to L.A.—so I couldn't relieve him.

"Fine. Are we almost there, wherever 'there' is?"

"Yeah, just take a right up here and then your first left." We rolled down the street and stopped in front of a faded storefront over which hung a startlingly bright wooden sign, the letters painted in amateurish strokes—the neon colors matched the lettering on the front of my new tank top.

"So this is Life Bytes," Hiro said, and cut the engine. "Can you enlighten me now?"

"There was a guy who used to hang around here who knew about all the yakuza action in L.A.—Shigeto. I'm hoping that he's here and that he'll know where Yoji's holed up. If not, I think Farnsworth can probably tell me where Shigeto lives."

"Farnsworth?" Hiro said with a tired smile. "That seems like almost too perfect a name for the assistant manager of an Internet café."

"Doesn't it?" I said, pushing open my door. "But he's a sweetheart. He had a crush on me when I was working here."

"But you only worked here for a week!" Hiro said, shucking off some of his tiredness.

"Less than that, actually . . . ," I said with a sigh. Hiro grabbed my arm.

33

"So how well do you know this Farnsworth guy?" he asked, pulling me back toward him. He was kidding around, but there was an unexpected undercurrent of seriousness in his voice.

"You're going to realize how silly this is when you meet him," I said, letting him pull me closer. "Besides, you were otherwise occupied back then, lest we forget."

Hiro put his fingers under my chin and tipped my head back.

"I've told you how things stand with Karen," he murmured, brushing a strand of hair off my face. "You know I think our relationship was a mistake—I told her that as soon as I realized it." He looked away for a moment. "She wasn't the person I thought she was," he added thoughtfully.

"I know," I said, melting into him a little more. "I'm just playing around." I hadn't realized how cold Karen was when I'd met her, either.

Hiro rumpled my hair. "Me too."

My heart thunked with love for him as we walked into Life Bytes, which was just as empty as I remembered it. Emptier, in fact. The place looked more run-down than ever, and no one had bothered to turn on the overhead lights. Dirty coffee cups and plates were stacked on the long Formica counter, and the recycling bins under the bank of printers were overflowing. To my dismay, I saw that the six computer terminals, each one stocked with a blueberry

Mac G4 and matching flat-screen monitor, were empty. No Shigeto. The place was dead except for the rippling glow of six geometric screen savers bouncing across the monitors.

"Farnsworth?" I called out tentatively.

A pale, bespectacled face poked out from behind the counter. Poor Farnsworth. His skin hadn't improved, and he still had the same unfortunate fashion sense as ever . . . no one had told him that turning the collar of your knit shirt up had gone out of style before we were born. (Not that I was one to talk, wearing that stupid tank top, but still. . . .) To make matters worse, he was wearing the hugest pair of headphones I'd ever seen, which made him look like a big, dorky insect. I stepped forward.

"Farnsworth, it's me," I said gently, holding out my hand.

"Huh-Huh-Heaven?" he stammered, pulling the headphones down onto his neck. "Whu-what are you doing here?"

Farnsworth's stuttering got worse when he was nervous. I walked over to the counter and sat down on one of the ripped red pleather bar stools.

"Who's that?" Farnsworth asked, nodding toward Hiro.

"I'm Hiro, a friend of Heaven's."

Hiro stood and offered Farnsworth his hand. For a moment it looked like Farnsworth would take it, but then he huddled against the back counter, ignoring Hiro's gesture.

35

"Is he one of *them*?" he asked me, looking at Hiro with a mixture of fear and distaste.

"Yakuza?" I said. "Definitely not."

"Whu-whu-why should I believe you?" Farnsworth asked.

"Because I'm telling you the truth," I said, looking at him steadily. "Actually, I'm looking for Shigeto," I added, figuring it was best just to get to the point.

Farnsworth raised a hand to his mouth and began gnawing at his fingernails.

"You cut your hair," he said finally, making it sound like an accusation. Suddenly a blast of techno music roared out of the speakers. Farnsworth jumped and ran back into the storeroom, where the stereo console was. Hiro perched on a stool next to mine.

"Quite a character," he yelled in my ear as the bass thumped around us. I nodded and tried to think about the best way to pry the information we needed out of Farnsworth.

The music cut off and Farnsworth slunk sheepishly back behind the counter. "Suh-sorry," he said. "I wuh-wuh-was working on a program to auto-organize my MP3 library. It's run into a few, uh, guh-glitches."

"Sounds pretty cool," I said, trying to feel out Farnsworth's vibe, as I remembered I was supposed to be using my heightened perception. He looked angry and scared. I glanced around the shop and wondered if the place was doing any business at all. Could that be one of the reasons Farnsworth was so pissed?

"He told me all about you, you know," Farnsworth said suspiciously, fiddling with a sugar packet. I remembered how awful the coffee had always been at Life Bytes—not that I'd been able to improve the quality during my brief employment.

"Shigeto?" I asked. Farnsworth nodded.

I sighed and tried to make eye contact with him, which was difficult. Whenever our eyes met, he looked away immediately. "I'm sorry I couldn't tell you, Farnsworth. And I'm sorry I had to bail on the job the way I did—but I didn't want to put you at risk. And I was in danger."

Farnsworth looked skeptical. I studied his face, and suddenly I realized—Farnsworth had been really *hurt* by my speedy departure. And even more hurt by the fact that I hadn't confided my situation to him. That Shigeto knew something about the world I was now involved in and Farnsworth didn't was a blow to his pride. The pissyness was just a cover. It was all right there on his face.

"Farnsworth," I said softly, "I really need to find Shigeto. He has information that I need. There are a lot of people after me, and I don't know who they are or where they are. If I can't find Shigeto, then I might not be able to get to the next piece of the puzzle."

"Wh-whu-what kind of information do you need? Sh-Shi-Shigeto's kind of out of it these days. He hasn't been here in weeks."

Patience, Heaven, I said to myself. I hadn't expected

such resistance from meek little Farnsworth—but I was learning that everyone had their limits.

"I need to know where a man named Yoji Yukemura is staying. His thugs have tried to kill me at least three times, and I want to ask him why."

"Can't you just Google him?" Farnsworth asked petulantly. "I mean, if he's such a powerful guy?"

"What do you think?" I snapped. Farnsworth cringed a little and pursed his lips. "Wherever he's hiding," I continued solicitously, trying to repair the damage, "it's so closely guarded, I'm not even sure Shigeto would know. But he might know someone who does."

"Wuh-well, I'm sorry i'm so stupid, Heaven, but, like, I'm just a hu-hu-humble Internet ca-café dork, not some, some hot-hotshot Japanese mafioso. Suh-sorry I can't help you out." Farnsworth slipped the headphones back on his head and turned to go.

"Farnsworth, wait!" I called, and slipped behind the counter. I backed him toward the wall and whispered, "Can we talk somewhere private?" Farnsworth's expression softened almost immediately, and his eyes darted around my face. "Like back there?" I continued, nodding toward the storeroom. Farnsworth gulped and nodded. "Lead the way," I said, then shot a last look at Hiro, who nodded approvingly.

"Listen," I said once we were alone, trying to make him feel like he was the only person in the whole world, "remember when I left Life Bytes? You asked me to let you know if I needed help. Well, I need it now. You're the only one who can help me to find . . . um . . . ," I stumbled, wanting to avoid using Shigeto's name, ". . . the key to what I'm looking for. Please, Farnsworth."

Farnsworth sat down on a folding chair and looked at me with puppy eyes magnified by thick glasses. I grabbed another chair and sat down across from him.

"Jeez, Heaven, you know I want to-to-to help you. But this yakuza stuff is just crazy. I mean, ever since I found out about you, I've been pretty scared about locking up at night—what if they find out I gave you Shigeto's address? They could, like, do some serious Buffy-style damage to me."

"Look," I said, glad that I was the pop culture addict I was, "just think of me as Buffy. I have a mission to complete, and although I have to keep it secret or it wouldn't be a mission, I still need help. You're like my Xander. And he was still standing after the final battle. Remember?"

"So is that guy Hiro your Angel?" Farnsworth asked sadly.

I blushed. Twenty-four hours had not been enough to acclimate me to the whole "couple" thing. "You're missing the point," I said, putting my hand on his arm. "I really, really need your help."

Farnsworth toyed with the headphones hanging around his neck. I kept my hand on his arm and told myself not to push it. I could feel that he was close to giving me the address. . . .

"It's on Bernard Street off Pioneer. I'm not sure of the exact address, but I know it's about halfway down the block and has a red door. I dropped him off there once. Pretty sketchy area."

"Farnsworth—you're the best!" I hugged him impulsively, then jumped up.

"Heaven," Farnsworth called plaintively, "duh-duh-do you think that, like, maybe if you ever cuh-complete your, you know, mission, that we could, like, huh-huh-huh . . ." His face turned red. "Hang out sometime?" he finished with a gasp.

"If I ever get myself out of this mess, I'd be honored to hang out with you." I ran for the door.

"Cool." Farnsworth grinned. "Oh, and I really like your hair."

"Thanks," I said, stopping short. "I've got to run," I explained apologetically.

"Go, go!" Farnsworth waved me away and turned back to his computer terminal. Out in front, Hiro stood staring out the window.

"Did you see something?" I asked, growing tense.

"I don't think so," Hiro said. "Did you get the address?"

I relaxed. "Yep. It's in Little Tokyo. Not too far."

As we pulled away from the curb, I thought about how I was pretty sure I would never see Farnsworth again and how sad that made me. Again I thought about whether I'd used him—but I'd had no choice. None of us did. Besides, even if I hadn't been in the crazy situation I was, it wasn't like Farnsworth and I would have been a couple.

I shook Farnsworth out of my thoughts—empathy was a luxury I couldn't afford right now. It was time to think about Shigeto.

4

By the time we got to Shigeto's neighborhood, it was dark. Honestly? Little Tokyo gave me the creeps. I'd had too many bad experiences there, starting with the last time I'd seen my adoptive father, Konishi—I'd agreed to meet him after hours at a restaurant, and a surprise ninja attack had put him in a coma from which, months later, he still hadn't emerged. It was weird—when I rolled down the window, the cool night air rolled into the car, carrying the smell of the sea. But not that good, wholesome, salty smell like you remember from the beach—it was more like the scent of all the dead things that had found their home at its bottom. I shuddered and rolled up the window.

"What's wrong?" Hiro asked, stretching a protective arm around my shoulders.

"It's probably nothing," I said, not wanting to sound like a baby.

"Come on, Heaven," Hiro chided. "You know better than that. It's time for you to start really trusting your instincts. If you sense something strange, it's for a reason."

I stared out the window and thought for a moment. "Something's not right here," I finally said. "It's like the streets around here are dead. I can smell it."

Hiro nodded. "I feel it, too. But I'm not sure I sense danger. Do you?"

I frowned. "No, it's not that—it's almost like whatever is lurking around here is long past being dangerous. Like, maybe it was a long time ago, but now it's just—" I searched for the right word "—decayed." Trying to put the feeling into words was frustrating. "I'm not sure if that's exactly what I mean," I added.

"I think I understand," Hiro said, slowing down at a stoplight. "You're feeling what anyone would in a neighborhood like this, if they took the time to process what they saw, heard, smelled—but most of us go around trying to pretend things are as normal as possible. We don't want to feel the danger lurking—to know we might be at risk."

"I'm not sure how I feel about this whole 'heightened perception' thing. It's too much information."

"It's a great responsibility. The more you pay attention to what your senses tell you, the closer you'll come to being

43

able to use your sixth sense—which is really just the answer to what the other five are trying to tell you."

I had to smile. "Okay, sensei," I joked. "I think I feel a lecture coming on."

"What, me? Lecture *you*?" Hiro drew down the corners of his mouth in mock seriousness. "Actually, there was a particularly apt story I was going to tell you about a warrior who failed to use his senses to gauge his surroundings. . . ."

"Ha ha," I said, then impulsively grabbed his hand. "Seriously, Hiro—it's nice to feel like we're working as a team now. Having you actually *help* me with my mission is a lot easier."

"Just let me know if I'm saying too much," Hiro said, squeezing my hand. "I don't mean to confuse you. As with every mission, you'll have to figure it out for yourself eventually."

"I know," I said, then sat up straight in my seat. "I think this is it."

In this part of the neighborhood, most of the streetlights were broken, and the ones that were left cast ominous shadows into the gaps between the ramshackle buildings. I could smell a fire burning somewhere not far from us, and I sensed the skitter of small animals (cats? rats?) running in and out of the dark alleys that radiated off Bernard. We tried a few buildings before we finally found Shigeto's—one of the worst on the block. The door *was* red, but just barely. You could hardly tell through the layer of dirt and scum.

The paint on the stairs was peeling off to reveal a rainbow of layers underneath. In the hallways lingered the stink of stale cooking, mixed with the smell of old cigarette smoke and a pinch of the dank sea scent I'd caught on the air outside. We climbed up to the third floor and headed down the dark hallway. I smelled pee and something else—puke? Somewhere a baby was crying. I made a mental note of the emergency door at the far end of the hallway—the exit sign wasn't lighted anymore, but I could make out the shape of the red letters hanging crookedly above the heavy metal door.

"Who's there?" came a muffled voice from inside. I looked at Hiro, and he touched my shoulder in support. I couldn't tell if the voice belonged to Shigeto or not.

"Heaven Kogo," I announced. From inside the apartment came the sound of scuffling, and then, without warning, the door opened with a sharp crack. Shigeto's eyes peered at me from behind the chain, but it was so dark, I couldn't make out his face.

"What do you want?" he demanded, his voice raspy and harsh.

"It's me, Heaven. I need to talk to you."

Shigeto's eyes darted from Hiro to me and back again, glowing like minnows in the half-light.

"Who's that?" he said, with a nod in Hiro's direction.

"This is my friend Hiro," I answered. Shigeto stared at him, unmoving. "He's okay," I added.

45

The door slammed. I stepped back, surprised.

"Ooo-kaaaay," Hiro said under his breath. A second later the door swung open.

"Come in, then," Shigeto mumbled, "and lock the door behind you."

Hiro and I stepped into a room so dark that it took my eyes a moment to adjust. The only light filtered in from the streetlamps outside. Shigeto stood with his back to the window, his shape making an eerie silhouette.

"Welcome to my little castle," he said. "It's not much, but it's safe." He flopped down onto one of several futons that filled up most of the floor space in the room, and when he leaned forward to grab a pack of cigarettes, his face came into the light for a moment.

I gasped. Shigeto, always a slender guy, had lost maybe thirty pounds since the last time I'd seen him. His face looked cavernous, and he'd grown a smattering of bedraggled facial hair. His microshort techno haircut had been replaced by a shaggy, dirty mane that he pushed agitatedly back behind his ears. I couldn't even begin to imagine what had happened to him.

"You got your hair cut," Shigeto said without interest, inhaling deeply on his cigarette.

"Looks like you let yours grow out," I answered.

"Yep," Shigeto said. I waited for him to continue.

"Well, now that we've dispensed with the formalities, why don't you tell me what the hell you want?"

Where was the slick, fun-loving DJ type I'd met at Life Bytes? *That* Shigeto had worn oversized jeans and told me he never touched anything more toxic than a glow stick when he went to dance clubs. The man sitting in front of me was a wreck—I watched as he stubbed out his cigarette in a half-crushed Schlitz can and lit another one.

"Would you mind if I opened a window?" Hiro asked. The room was smoky and far too warm. I was desperate for some of that cool California night air, even if it did smell like rotting seaweed. Shigeto's place smelled like—*animals*. As though he hadn't left for weeks.

Shigeto shrugged. "Whatever gets your groove on, man. I aim to please." He stared at me. "So, you gonna talk, or did you just come over to chill out in my phat pad?" he asked, his voice dripping with sarcasm.

Hiro stood up and slid open one of the dirty windows. I breathed the cool air in deeply.

"I need some information and I thought you could help me," I said simply. Something told me it was wiser not to tell Shigeto what I was after until I'd figured out where we stood and what had happened since I'd last seen him.

"What kind of information could a *Kogo* possibly need from me?" Shigeto spit out my name like he'd just eaten a fly or something. I was tongue-tied for a moment. I hadn't expected such venom from Shigeto. I studied his face just as I had studied Farnsworth's—his eyes were narrowed, lips curled. I allowed my eyes to slide from his face and scanned the little room, so dirty and decrepit, so unsuitable for any human being to be living in—and suddenly I just knew: not only did he know everything about me and my family, but he *hated* us.

"I gather that you understand something of what's going on . . . ," I started.

Shigeto loudly blew out a stream of smoke. "I don't know *nothing*, man. I don't *know* nothing, and I don't *want* to know nothing."

Fear. I could sense it coming from him. He was worried. I wondered if he was afraid of what the Yukemuras might do to him—or of what they *had* done.

It occurred to me that maybe it was the Kogos he was worried about.

"It's okay, Shigeto," I soothed. "No one even knows I'm in L.A. We just need a few more minutes of your time and then we'll go."

"A few minutes of my time might be too much," Shigeto said. He crawled over a few futons to a minirefrigerator propped clumsily against the wall and pulled out a can of Miller High Life. "The Champagne of Beers," he said, twisting off the cap with a snort. He took a long pull off the bottle, then wiped his mouth with the back of his hand. "You Kogos are bad news. And I don't want anything to do with you."

"What are you talking about, exactly?" I asked, treading lightly.

"How can you ask me what *I'm* talking about? You think I'm stupid? You think I don't know that there's a price on your head?" Shigeto's voice was growing more agitated, and his eyes darted wildly around the room, the whites gleaming in the half-light from the street. "Give me one reason why I shouldn't call Yoji Yukemura right now and tell him to send over some of his yakuza to pick you up. The money I'd make would get me out of this craphole, that's for sure." Shigeto held up his cell phone, his finger poised above the keypad.

I glanced at Hiro. The bounty being offered for my capture was news to me. Hiro raised his eyebrows but didn't speak. He didn't look too shocked, either.

"Why does Yoji Yukemura want me?" I asked. Maybe Shigeto knew more than I'd expected.

Shigeto rolled his eyes. "Are you kidding? Everyone who's anyone knows about the Kogo-Yukemura feud. Sounds to me like your daddy grew himself a big ol' swelled head—giant size. He thought if he could convince Yoji to let you marry his son, then he could stage a ninja attack and get rid of all the Yukemuras at once. Too bad things didn't go the way he planned. First his son bought it, and now he's halfway to dead himself." Shigeto paused. "But you know all that."

I clenched my fists. As sorry as I felt for Shigeto, hearing him accuse my father of those things filled me with rage. It was true I had once wondered about my father's role in the ninja attack, but now I was almost certain he'd had nothing to do with it. Although they had their differences, he'd loved Ohiko, who was his only biological child.

"Who's saying those things?" I demanded. "Is that what people really think?"

"What *people*?" Shigeto said, mocking me. "It's not like it was in the *L.A. Times* or nothing. The *people* I know get that's what happened. So the way I see it, old man Yoji's got a pretty damn good reason for wanting to round you up."

"Listen to me, Shigeto," I said, trying to keep my voice even. "That's a lie. Yoji Yukemura knows who sent the ninjas to attack the wedding—and it wasn't my father. That's why I need to talk to him. Besides, if you know as much as you say you do about yakuza, then you know it's my responsibility to go make peace. Ohiko can't do it, and Konishi can't do it, so that leaves me. I need to know where I can find him."

Shigeto slurped at his beer and used his long, dirty fingernails to pick pieces of stuffing out of the futon on which he sprawled. He lit yet another cigarette. "Why should I tell you anything?" he asked sulkily. I sensed that his bravado was just that—a way for him to play tough. He had nothing against me, and I doubted he even believed the stories he was telling about the Kogos. There was something else Shigeto wanted—I just couldn't figure out what yet. I'd have to open up if I wanted to find out.

"Because Teddy Yukemura is dead," I said. "We were

there when he was killed. Whoever's trying to kill me is the same person who killed my brother and put my father in a coma. Yoji's going to want to know who's responsible for his son's death, don't you think?" I paused for effect, then let loose with my wild card: "And I don't think Yoji would be happy to hear that Heaven Kogo wasn't able to deliver some very important news to him because some former DJ named Shigeto wouldn't cough up a little information that a hundred people already know—where Yoji's staying."

That got his attention. Shigeto stood up and drew the curtains. "Tell me what happened," he said, "and maybe I'll have some information for you. Maybe."

I told the story as quickly as possible, and occasionally Hiro jumped in to quietly clarify or add something I'd forgotten. We were quite a team. But during the entire story, Shigeto couldn't keep still. He wandered around the tiny studio, pulling out candles from overflowing drawers, under piles of books, and between the cracks of the futons, and lit them one after the other. By the time I was done, the room was filled with an eerie, flickering light and the smell of burnt matches. For the first time I could see the tattered posters on the wall: Mulder and Scully, standing back to back, guns drawn, under a caption that said "The Truth Is Out There." The little girl from *Spirited Away* surrounded by Miyazaki's magical creatures. A pinup of Heidi Klum in a bikini. And the walls around them were filthy— yellowed from the smoke and stained brown with who knew what. I pictured the little studio as it must have been when Shigeto had first moved in—he was probably proud of his decorating back then.

It hurt too much to look at the posters—they were remnants of the Shigeto I'd met at Life Bytes, and that Shigeto was gone now. I gazed instead at the tiny flames of the flickering candles and waited for his response. As I looked at the bright points of light, I felt something sort of pop inside me, and with a rush I could suddenly feel all of Shigeto's pent-up thoughts and feelings. The room was thick with them. It was as though my brain had finally allowed itself to compute all the facts I'd taken in since setting foot in the building and was finally ready to spit out the answers. I understood that Shigeto was using drugs and that he'd been beaten for something—what, exactly, I couldn't tell, but the way he hunched over gingerly on his futon, the crusted bits of blood around his hairline, barely visible unless you really looked—they told the story as well as Shigeto could have. Drug debts? Something else? I knew that since I'd seen him at Life Bytes, he'd become involved with the yakuza (a hint of a tattoo peeked from the bottom of his sleeve), and I knew that he regretted it and was scared for his life.

"What's your last name, Shigeto?" I asked quietly.

"Kimura," he whispered, squirming a little on his futon.

"Your father's name is Sadakuzo," I said, pleased at the part of my brain that was bringing forth this long-forgotten knowledge, calmed by the feeling of my mind working with such precision and so little emotion. "I remember him visiting from America when I was young. Isn't that right?"

Pain. I felt it when Shigeto's eyes caught mine. "He's dead. They killed him," he said flatly.

I nodded.

"He wasn't even yakuza!" Shigeto yelled in a high-pitched voice. "He was just a businessman! They convinced him to transfer some of their funds through his offshore accounts. Like, half a billion dollars or something. And he did it and they suckered him. They just freaking shot him after the money came through. Didn't want to leave a trail—you people are devils!"

"I'm sorry, Shigeto," I said. "I really am. Believe me, I don't want anything more to do with these people than you do."

"Once a Kogo, always a Kogo. You people just take whatever you want and don't give a shit who dies along the way." Shigeto was curled up against the wall and fighting back tears.

"You're confused, Shigeto. You don't know what to believe or who to turn to," I intoned, not sure exactly where the words were coming from. I only knew that in that moment, I felt an intense connection with the sad man in front of me who'd been broken almost beyond recognition. "You think that maybe the Yukemuras will help you avenge your father's death. But they could just as easily kill you."

53

"What are you doing?" Shigeto gasped, his eyes wide. His fingers clutched wildly at his hair.

"Part of you wants us to get out of your apartment so you can shoot up some more, and the other part of you is glad to have someone around to witness what you've become. You want to tell us who did this to you, but you're scared—"

"Stop! Stop!" screamed Shigeto.

"Heaven, that's enough!" Hiro cautioned. "He's not well."

I clamped my mouth shut. The thing inside me that had popped open closed itself with a snap. What had I done?

"This is so messed up, so messed up," repeated Shigeto, rocking back and forth. "You were totally in my head, man, in my *head*. That's not *right*."

I looked at Hiro, who was staring at me intensely. I didn't know what to say. I had totally freaked Shigeto out—a stupid mistake. Just because I'd been able to use my perception to figure out the scenario didn't mean I had to let the whole world know about it. And Shigeto was certainly not ready to be confronted with the truth of his situation. I prayed I hadn't scared him too badly.

"Here," he said, jumping up and scrabbling on a nearby table for paper and a pen. He scribbled for a moment and then threw the piece of paper at me. "You can find Yoji there. Just take it and get out."

"Shigeto, I—"

"Get out!" he screamed, and turned his face toward the wall.

Hiro helped me up and I made my way shakily down the hallway. When we got to the stairwell, panic rose in my chest, and I felt that I would die if I had to spend one more second breathing the foul air of that building. I bolted down the stairs.

"Heaven! Wait!"

I burst out into the open, gasping for air, devouring it in delicious gulps. Hiro came up behind me and put his hand gently on my back.

"Are you okay?" he asked.

"That was too intense," I whispered.

"You opened a new door with your perception. . . . It was quite amazing, really. Normally it takes people years to get to that level." Hiro put his arm around me. "It's draining, isn't it?" he asked sympathetically.

I nodded, cuddling against him. "That was *not* my idea of a good time."

"Wasn't it nice to see things so clearly, though?" Hiro said soothingly, his hand warm on my back.

"Yeeess," I said slowly. "When all the wheels are turning together, it feels pretty amazing. But I think I went too far."

"You'll get the hang of it," Hiro said, sounding every inch the proud sensei. "So where's Yoji?"

I fished the paper out of my pocket. "Hotel Bel-Air. Presidential suite." I stared at the paper. Next to the English writing was the word *fire* written in Japanese. *What?* I crumpled the paper. I couldn't think about what the symbol might mean right now.

"What is it?" Hiro asked, opening the car door for me.

"I'm scared," I said.

"Let's get out of here," Hiro said, giving me a quick peck on the cheek. He started the engine and soon we were driving away from Little Tokyo. "What do you say we head back to my place? We could take a nap, get cleaned up—I don't think we should be confronting Yoji in this condition."

"Sounds good," I lied. As soon as Hiro mentioned his house on Lily Place, I had a strange feeling of unease. But he was right. We needed some rest or we'd be useless.

"Don't worry, Heaven," Hiro said gently. "New skills hurt at first—but when you master them, you can't imagine what it would have been like to live without them."

5

As soon as I stepped out onto the pavement in front of Hiro's house, I knew something was wrong. I stopped short at the foot of the walkway. Hiro looked back at me.

"You feel it?" he asked, concern flitting over his face.

"It's weird—I do, but I don't think there's anyone else here. It's more like I know something bad has happened."

"How do you know?" Hiro grilled me.

I listened. All I could hear was the soft chirping of the crickets and the shush-shush of the neighborhood's sprinklers. I shrugged. "Beats me. I'm just getting a bad vibe."

"Maybe it's this?" Hiro picked up a black glove from halfway down the walkway and gestured in the air with it.

"Oh. Yeah." I grinned sheepishly.

"And do you smell the air? It smells like cigar smoke. Here . . ." Hiro leaned over and fished a cigar stub out of the grass that lined the path. "Someone was here recently."

"Guess I missed that," I said, blushing. So much for my triumphant career as a mind-reading machine.

"No, you didn't. You caught it, and that's why you got a 'bad vibe.' You just didn't realize what you had seen and smelled. But you have to be able to know what signs you're reading and read them the right way." Hiro dropped the glove and the cigar butt and walked back toward me, wiping his hands on his jeans. "How do you feel?" he whispered. "I mean, are you rested enough to fight if we need to?"

"Yes," I said, although I wasn't so sure.

"Good. Let's go around the side."

Hiro led the way around the side of the house, and we slunk behind the bushes and along the wall toward the back door. A magnolia tree bloomed in the neighbors' yard—I inhaled deeply and prayed that my intuition was right and there wasn't someone waiting inside to attack us.

Hiro hopped onto the back patio, nodded in my direction, and quickly threw open the door. We jumped inside almost in unison, both standing in the ready position. The smell—no, it wasn't a real scent, it was a *psychic* smell, really, the way the place felt in my head—anyway, it was bad. It was violent. Images of anger, dark purple, bruised, ugly, flashed before my eyes. It was too dark to look for signs, so I focused on staying calm. Hiro moved out into the living room and I followed him carefully. Something crunched under our feet. It was dark. The tiny house was empty. Hiro flipped on a light.

"Oh, no," I breathed. The place had been ransacked. Sofa cushions slashed, clothes on the floor, everything that could be broken, stomped, ripped, stained, trashed, dashed *was*—just a totally thorough, Hollywood-style search. Which was funny, actually, because we were *in* Hollywood. The thought failed to amuse me, though. It just reminded me that once upon a time, in my other life, I had been a total movie buff. I couldn't even imagine having time for that now.

"What were they looking for?" I asked, peeking into the bedroom. They'd destroyed the altar where Hiro meditated, and his red Japanese candles lay strewn across the floor amid the splinters of the kuden, or inner sanctuary.

"I don't think they were looking for anything." Hiro shook his head. "They're trying to send a message."

I reached over to pick up the pieces of the altar, tears pricking my eyes.

"Heaven," cautioned Hiro. I drew my hand back. "I don't think we should touch anything we don't have to."

"Why not? They're gone."

"It's just not safe. We should get out of here as quickly as possible. I'm going to grab some clothes and stuff."

"Should we go to a motel?" I asked, feeling more at loose ends than I had all day.

"Still risky," Hiro said. He thought for a minute. "How

59

about the dojo? We can shower there. We can even brush up on our moves before we head over to the Bel-Air."

"Sounds good," I said, and watched as Hiro started to search through the mess for some clean clothes. I leaned my head against the wall and sighed. I felt terrible. The house on Lily Place had been such a haven. It was tiny and cozy, and it was the first place I'd stayed after the wedding. The weeks we'd lived there, just Hiro and I, had been so hard, yet so amazing. Even as I'd tried to come to terms with Ohiko's death and all that had happened, a whole new world had been opening up to me.

And now that new world was crumbling.

"I'm sorry, Hiro," I said.

"For what?" he asked, then held up a duffel bag he'd salvaged. "Bingo!"

"For this," I said, waving my hand vaguely. "I know how hard you worked to make a place for yourself. And now it's all ruined."

Hiro stopped searching for clothes. "Heaven, don't think like that," he said. "This is all meaningless, really. Just things, easily replaced. If they hadn't trashed the house, then we'd still be in exactly the same situation we were before. It doesn't change anything."

"But you have nothing to come home to now!" I wailed, feeling like a baby but unable to stop myself.

"We'll just have to build a home together," Hiro said, looking away. My heart caught in my throat. I stepped behind him and tentatively draped my arms around his shoulders. I wasn't sure if it was the right thing to do; I only knew that I felt like doing it. I pressed my chest against Hiro's back and felt a tremor run through his frame. With one sweeping motion that was more samurai than boyfriend, he flipped me in front of him and pressed me up against the bedroom wall. His hands ran over my body and we kissed hungrily. Warmth flowed through my chest and I fell out of time, raised to some delicious other plane of existence where the only goal was for Hiro and me to get closer and closer.

Hiro wrenched himself away. I opened my eyes and blinked twice. "What happened?" I asked. "Did I do something wrong?"

"Definitely, *definitely* not," Hiro said, reaching out to touch my face but otherwise keeping his distance. "Everything was too right. But it's still not safe here." He looked around. "I think there's one more thing we need before we leave, though."

I watched shakily as he dragged a chair into the bedroom closet, hurling clothes and cushions out of his way as he went. I'd never thought a kiss could feel quite like *that*.

"What are you doing?" I asked. This was no time for housecleaning. He wedged the chair into the closet, whose floor was littered with sparring pads, hopped on top, and reached his arms far into the deepest, highest corner.

Hiro grunted, straining on tiptoe. Then he came out,

smiling. "Looks like they weren't as thorough as they thought."

It was the Whisper of Death. My family's katana—the samurai sword I'd taken when I fled from the wedding.

"They didn't find it," I whispered, taking it gently from Hiro's hands. It felt good to hold it again. When I wrapped my hands around its hilt, I felt like the sword was speaking to me, telling me everything would be okay.

"We'll take it with us," Hiro said, and I nodded, sitting down on the couch with the Whisper in my lap while Hiro collected some clothes and his toothbrush.

Soon we were ready to go. An awkward silence hung between us—I was thinking about what he'd said, about building a life together, and I knew he was, too. Even though he'd already said, "I love you," having Hiro tell me that he wanted to be with me no matter what, after all this was over (if it ever ended), seemed more serious. More concrete.

"Ready?" Hiro said.

"Always." I smiled.

A blast of cool air hit my face as we pushed through the cherry-wood doors and made our way into the dojo. The iron wind chimes that hung above the doorway announced our arrival. I leaned against the reception counter and eagerly breathed in the fresh, sandalwood-scented air. The dojo had been a sanctuary for me since the moment I'd first set foot there, and one look at Hiro's face—the frown lines on his brow now relaxed, the tension gone from his jaw— was enough to tell me he felt the same way.

"Oh my God! Hey, you guys!" Sami, my favorite instructor at the dojo, came jogging down the hallway, gray eyes sparkling, her blond hair piled in a bun on top of her head. "Is everything okay?"

I hugged Sami, grateful that someone, at least, was happy to see me. She was tall and strong, a good hugger.

"We're fine," I said. "We just need to get cleaned up." Sami looked us over, her smile fading. "Are you in trouble?" she whispered, looking from me to Hiro and back again. "You guys changed your hair. . . ."

"It's okay, Sami," Hiro said. "Don't worry about us. We just need to hang out here for a few hours, if that's all right."

"Of course it's all right," Sami said. She glanced over her shoulder. "But Karen's here. . . ."

Crap. One thing I most certainly didn't need was a Karen sighting. The last time we'd seen each other, things had almost devolved into an all-out fistfight—and that was *before* Hiro broke up with her.

"I mean, it might be kind of, um, weird if she sees you two together here," Sami whispered, looking at us apologetically. "I know it's none of my business, but she told me you guys broke up," she said to Hiro.

Hiro nodded, his face blank. I could tell he was assessing the situation.

63

"Maybe I'll just grab a shower, and you can go talk to Karen, let her know we're here," I said. The truth was, my jealousy of Karen had evaporated as soon as Hiro had expressed his feelings for me. I felt kind of sorry for her, actually. But that didn't mean it would be a good idea to see her.

"Sounds like a plan," Hiro said.

"I'll grab you some towels." Sami ducked behind the reception desk. I was about to follow her into the storeroom, but something inspired me to turn around and give Hiro a flirty wave. Big mistake.

"Hello, Hiro." Karen was striding down the hallway toward us. Just then Sami reemerged from the storeroom with a stack of towels in her arms. She looked from Karen to Hiro to me, then froze.

"Um . . . I've got to go clean out the sauna," Sami said nervously, pushing the towels toward me. "See you guys! Nice hair!" she chirped, turning red.

Karen stared straight at Hiro, making no sign that she even saw me there. She looked awful—for her, anyway. To anyone who didn't know her, she'd still probably have been drop-dead gorgeous. But her normally glowing skin was pale and slack, and she had dark circles under her eyes.

"Back so soon?" Karen said, and gave a little snort.

"Hello, Karen," Hiro said.

"I'm just going to go take a shower," I chimed in, wishing the floor would open up and swallow me. Ninjas—no problem. A drug den in Little Tokyo—no problem. But one look at Karen had taken all the fight right out of me.

"Don't leave on *my* account," Karen said, still not looking at me. "After all, I'm sure Hiro doesn't keep any secrets from you."

I looked at Hiro, hoping to take my cue from him, but he wasn't looking at me. I felt about three inches tall.

"Do you want to talk?" Hiro asked.

"It's a little late for that," Karen sneered, leaning against the front desk. "But I guess you could answer one question for me. Just something I've been wondering about. How does Heaven feel about dating a guy who runs off to Vegas without a word? Who can treat you like a queen but secretly be lusting after someone else the whole time?"

"I'm sorry you got hurt, but we've already talked about this," Hiro said gently. "Oh, *I* didn't get hurt," Karen said, her voice hard and bitter, "but your little fighting doll over here might if she sticks with you."

"How can you say that about me?" I interrupted, unable to keep my mouth shut. I couldn't just stand there and let her talk about me as if I didn't exist. "You know that's not true!"

"What?" Karen asked, feigning surprise. "You mean it's not true that you're a scheming, conniving, manipulative little bitch who goes around stealing people's boyfriends?"

"Karen!" Hiro snapped, his voice stern. "That's enough!"

"I'm just telling it like it is," Karen hissed, "and if you

can't deal with that, you better get out of here and take your little protégé with you. You've got a helluva lot of nerve showing up here. And that platinum hair doesn't suit you. Was that her contribution to your new 'look'?"

"This is unacceptable," Hiro said harshly. "I admit I wasn't one hundred percent honest with you, but it was only because I wasn't being honest with myself. Heaven has nothing to do with it, and she certainly doesn't deserve your insults."

I wanted to jump in again, but I held back. Having Hiro defend me to Karen made me feel weird—on the one hand, I was glad he was sticking up for me. But the independent Heaven who had been born since I came to the States wasn't crazy about it. Still, I had the feeling piping up just now would only make things worse.

"Well, it looks like Heaven's found herself a little protector. You play the role to the hilt, don't you, Hiro?"

"I think this conversation is over," Hiro said, turning away.

"It's not over!" Karen yelled, her face contorting for a moment. "I deserve some answers!"

"What kind of answers do you want, exactly?" Hiro asked, facing her again. I could tell he was trying not to shout. "There's nothing more I can tell you. I said I'm sorry, and—"

"Sorry's not enough!" Karen interrupted.

"I'm out of here," I said. I couldn't take it anymore.

They were going in circles, and it really had nothing to do with me.

"Good!" Karen snapped. "No one wants you around anyway."

I ground my teeth together and stared down at the geometric pattern of the light wood floor. *Don't rise to the bait, Heaven,* I told myself. The question was, how could this strong, powerful woman be acting like a thirteen-year-old girl? Call me naive about these things, but it was mind-boggling. Especially considering Karen could probably date anyone she wanted to without even lifting a finger.

"Stop acting like a child," Hiro said. "You're embarrassing yourself."

"Screw you, Hiro. And you too," Karen added, flashing a glance in my direction. "I don't need this bullshit." Karen grabbed her bag and stormed out of the dojo.

Hiro stood quietly. I sensed that whatever he was feeling (guilt? regret?), he needed to deal with it on his own. I slipped off to the locker room and almost fell asleep under the hot pounding of the shower water. I had felt Karen's anger, her sense of betrayal, but there was nothing I could do about it. I didn't feel guilty—not about her. She'd been too mean for that. I let the water wash away the imprint of her words, and by the time I was pulling on the clean T-shirt Hiro had brought for me and a pair of gi pants I'd borrowed from the front desk, I'd almost forgotten the whole ugly scene. I had more important things to think about. Like Yoji Yukemura.

I wandered out into the hallway, scanning the rows of sliding rice-paper doors for some indication of which room Hiro was using. I could hear the rhythmic thumps and shouts of a few classes going on, and for a second I closed my eyes and let the familiar, muted clatter soothe me.

"In here!" Hiro called out to me from one of the practice rooms. I stepped in and slid the door shut.

"I'm really sorry about that," he said shyly, taking me in his arms gently, not like back at the house. I could smell the clean scent of soap on his skin. His white-blond hair was slicked back—I had to giggle. It was almost as if he had become one of those Japanese hipsters who flooded the Shibuya district, running around in James Dean outfits— hair slicked back with grease, combs in the back pockets of their vintage 501s, old-school leather biker jackets.

"Forget about it," I breathed. I glanced up at him and cracked up again. "You need to make your hair into more of a ducktail to complete the look."

"What?" Hiro looked confused. He wasn't exactly on the cutting edge of popular culture—much less popular culture recycled from fifty years ago.

"Never mind," I said, enjoying the feeling of his strong arms around me. Hiro put his hands on my face and tilted it up so he could look in my eyes.

"I want you to know that none of that stuff means any- thing to me. I feel sorry for Karen, but I tried to be honest with her. And I will *always* be honest with you."

"I know," I said, melting against him. He leaned his face toward me and our lips met. We kissed slowly this time, deeply. I ran my hands over his back as he drew me to him, our bodies pressed together. Hiro wrapped one arm around my waist and tenderly touched my cheek with the other, and we kept kissing. I felt like I was falling into a deep pool, and I worried that I would never make it back to the surface. This time it was me who finally pulled away, catching my breath.

"It's too intense," I said. "I'm sorry." I could feel the love and passion emanating from Hiro in waves. What might happen if we kept going frightened me. Not in a bad way, exactly, but it was still scary. I just couldn't do it.

"I understand," he said, kissing my cheek and neck slowly. "The connection is amazing." He planted a kiss on my forehead and released me. I slid onto the floor and he sat down next to me, his arm around my shoulders.

"Are you ready?" Hiro asked, looking into my eyes. "Not just for the fight, but for what you might learn?"

I stared into his eyes, and suddenly my mind was flooded with visions of my life "before." I thought about my "normal" childhood, how peaceful it had been back before I knew that I was different from other children, before my father began to make demands on Ohiko and me that threatened to make our sheltered world even smaller, before death entered the Kogo house, and before the truth began to seep out and soil everything that I'd known. It felt amazing to have Hiro and to know that he was willing to stand next to me while I fulfilled my duty to my family. Looking back, I could see that he had never wavered. But was I ready to learn who was really after me, even if the answer was something I didn't want to hear?

"Yes," I breathed. I was ready. As ready as I'd ever be.

"Good," Hiro said, leaping up and holding out his hand. "Let's prepare."

I took his hand. I was ready to kick some ass.

Unbelievable. I'm sitting in my car, trying to stop my hands from shaking so I can get out of here, drive as far away as possible from Hiro and that horrible Heaven. What a pair. They really deserve each other.

I'm too good for him.

So why does it hurt so much?

I just—I regret the day he walked into my dojo. I let down my guard, let myself believe that he was different from all the others. But he was just the same.

A little deep breathing—that's good. I need to get control of myself. As I pull into traffic, though, I feel that the rage is still there. He threw me out like a piece of trash. One minute it was all, 'Karen, you are my lotus flower, my calm center,' and the next minute—boom. He's off to Joshua Tree to rescue Little Miss Heaven from her latest disaster.

I'm tired of playing the victim, the innocent bystander. As if it weren't enough that I was kidnapped in her place by mistake, now I'm supposed to be totally fine with the fact that she's stolen my boyfriend. Like I'm the psycho in this equation. I don't think so.

When the three men showed up at my house after Hiro left, I was scared at first. I wanted nothing to do with whatever Heaven had gotten herself into. But if what they told me was true, then Hiro isn't the person I thought he was—and that means he was lying to me all along. I'm not sure what to believe, but something tells me those guys were telling the truth. They were very polite. Well spoken. Tailored suits—silk, classic styling. They knew details of Hiro's life that would be hard to learn, like how he lived in the YMCA when he first came to the States and was learning English, and how he traveled to Kyoto during the Kurama Torch Festival in order to determine what path to take in his life, and how he studied in one of the oldest dojos there for almost a year before returning to Tokyo and packing his things to come to the U.S.

I'd always hoped we'd travel back there together.

Oh God, it drives me mad when I think of the things he said! How dare he chastise me for criticizing Heaven? As if he didn't always complain about how immature and uncommitted to her training she was? As if he didn't tell me a hundred times that he wasn't sure if he could help her and didn't know if he even ought to? Was it all just a ruse so that I wouldn't suspect anything? And if he could lie to me like that, then why should I believe the other things he told me about Heaven's situation? Not that he told me much. That's what I keep coming back to, what makes me think those men were telling the truth—and that Hiro and Heaven are dangerous and headed for trouble. If I don't do something, somebody else is going to get hurt—badly.

The truth is, I don't owe him anything. I need to do what I can to protect myself. No one else is going to. It feels like

L.A. is over for me. So I'll make the call, do the right thing, take the money, and head back to San Francisco. I just want to put all this behind me—and I should get out of this nightmare with something for myself.

    Right?

    Right.

Karen

6

The Hotel Bel-Air was nothing like the Beverly Wilshire.

"Is this it?" I asked Hiro as he pulled the car into a parking lot nestled among the trees. "This looks like a park."

"Come on, Heaven," Hiro chided. "I thought you'd know all about this place from your celebrity addiction—this is where big stars like Brad Pitt go for privacy."

"Why, Hiro," I said, feigning shock, "you know who Brad Pitt is?" I slammed my car door shut and we walked toward the reception house, which looked more like some superstar's private villa than a hotel. But I guess that was the point. "This is so different from the Beverly Wilshire," I said as we stepped into the lobby. "But I think I remember this place now. Isn't this where they have all those little individual bungalows for people? And wasn't there that movie where—?"

"Later, Heaven," Hiro said, cautioning me. I snapped my mouth shut. "Concentrate on feeling out your surroundings."

"Feels pretty swanky," I muttered.

"What?"

"Never mind." I scanned the lobby. A high ceiling soared above the room, and one whole wall was actually constructed of two huge glass doors that opened up onto a patio. Candles flickered on small tables throughout the lobby and out on the Spanish tiles of the patio, and comfortable-looking love seats and chaises littered the place, which was empty except for two men at the reception desk. I grabbed Hiro's arm.

"We're not going to get anywhere with those two."

"I agree," Hiro said, and we ducked quietly out onto the patio and into the darkness of the trees. The smell of flowers was sweet and heavy.

"How are we going to find Yoji's suite?" I asked, taking in the vast gardens. You could see pinpoints of light from the various guest bungalows, but not much more. "This place looks like it goes on forever."

"Well, the presidential suite is probably the biggest."

"Right. And the best guarded."

"We're just going to have to sleuth it out," Hiro said, slipping into the darkness. I followed him in and out of the shadows, letting him lead the way. In between focusing as hard as I could on which paths we were taking and committing them to memory, I imagined running into Colin Farrell or Nicole Kidman and scaring the hell out of them. I could see the cover of the *Enquirer* now: HOLLYWOOD HOTTIES' HOT DATE CRASHED BY ROGUE SAMURAI!

"That's it," Hiro whispered, stopping short. I bumped into his back and out of my reverie. Rubbing my nose, I stared through the leaves and saw two dark shapes patrolling back and forth on the patio of a bungalow slightly larger than the others.

"Do you think Yoji's here?" I asked. The windows of the bungalow were dark.

Hiro shrugged. "We have to try." He stepped out onto the path, and I followed.

"We're here to see Yoji Yukemura," he said, holding up his hands to show he was unarmed.

The two shapes froze, and I saw the dark outline of two hands reaching for two hips—I prayed that Hiro had the right idea about our entrance.

"How did you get up here?"

The shapes came into the light, and I saw that neither of the guards was Japanese, which was out of the ordinary—normally someone as high-level yakuza as Yoji would use only the most trusted family retainers for his personal safety detail.

"I want to see Yoji Yukemura," I said simply, stepping in front of Hiro.

The bodyguard stared at me for a second, then burst

into laughter. "She wants to see Mr. Yukemura, Joe," he called over his shoulder to his cohort. Joe walked up, all six foot six inches of him, it looked like, and chuckled.

"Well, no problem, Stevenson," he said sarcastically. "Why don't you just let the lady and her friend right in?" They cracked up, but I didn't move. Stevenson wiped his eyes and crossed his humongous arms in front of him. He wore an electric blue suit and a heavy silver bracelet, and I could see a tattoo peeking out from under the collar of his shirt. I wondered if these two had been indoctrinated into the yakuza or if they were just a couple of Hells Angels or something. Was Yoji that desperate for security?

"Take that little path right back where you came from, girlie. And take your boyfriend with you. Mr. Yukemura's busy."

"Tell him it's Heaven Kogo who wants to see him," I said.

Instantly the smiles disappeared. Joe and Stevenson moved forward as if to grab me, but Hiro stepped between us.

"Stop," he said, his voice cold and menacing. "We're here, we're unarmed, and we want to see Yoji Yukemura. Go let him know."

Joe cleared his throat. "Better frisk them, Stevenson. I'll go tell Mr. Yukemura." Joe slipped behind the door and Stevenson ran his hands over us, looking for weapons.

"Watch it," Hiro cautioned as Stevenson's hands lingered

a moment too long on my thigh. I sighed. I'd become ridiculously used to such things while I was working as a shot girl at Vibe—another short-lived stint.

Joe reemerged. He nodded and the two bodyguards led us into the suite. The rooms were dark, and it was hard to get a handle on where the exits were. The air smelled damp, as though someone had just taken a shower. As my eyes adjusted, I saw oversized furniture and a set of glass doors just like in the lobby, except smaller—and these were locked, a steel bar lowered across them. Just beyond the glass, a blue pool lit from within glittered like a giant aquamarine. I still didn't sense any danger, although logic told me I ought to. We were in the dragon's lair—but it felt like any other fancy hotel room, placid and sumptuous.

Stevenson gestured to the couch and Hiro and I sat down next to each other. A shadow emerged from the room next door, and with a shock I realized that the hunched-over figure was Yoji Yukemura. He had aged years since the wedding.

"Thank you, Joe, thank you, Stevenson, that will be all," he said, his voice rusty and broken. The bodyguards stepped back out into the hallway and Yoji sat down across from us in a heavy leather armchair. His posture telegraphed frustration and sadness—it wasn't hard to sense, but at least I was finally gathering some information I could use.

"I've lost two of my men trying to get ahold of you," Yoji

said raspily, "and now you've walked right into my hands."
He paused, selecting a cigar from a cedar box and clipping
the end off neatly. "Why are you here?"

"We were with Teddy when he was killed," I said.

"Do you think I'm not aware of that?" he asked, lighting
his cigar with a long wooden match. His voice was even,
expressionless. "That can't be all you came to tell me."

"No," I said, surprised to find that I felt sorry for a man
I'd considered my enemy for so long. "I came here with
questions to ask. But I wanted you to know that I cared
about Teddy. I know you might not believe it," I pressed on
as Yoji puffed on his cigar, "but at times over the past few
months he's been the only person I could count on who
understood exactly what I was going through."

"What about your young friend?" Yoji asked, gesturing
toward Hiro.

"It's different," I said. "Teddy and I were both stuck—
our families used us to get what they wanted. We had nothing to do with what was happening to us." Yoji raised his
eyebrows and stared at Hiro, his eyes narrowing. He
opened his mouth as if to say something, then closed it
again and contemplated his cigar instead.

"With Takeda gone, you are useless to me. You knew
that when you decided to come here."

"So why have you put a price on my head? Why are your
men out looking for me?" I asked, more confused than ever.

"Street talk," Yoji said huskily, waving my words away.

"As soon as I heard about the disaster in Mexico, I called my men off. You've been followed since you both entered the city, it's true, but just as a precaution. As I said, with Takeda missing, how can I join our families when there is nothing to join? *I*, alas, remain married to Takeda's mother, a formidable woman. So you see, I am unavailable for the task. Takeda was our only son—*is* our only son, I should say, since my men have not yet been able to recover a body."

"I'm sorry, Yoji-san," I said, "but I believe Teddy is dead. I saw them shoot him." My voice trembled, but I pressed on. Yoji *had* to understand what was at stake. "He fell to the ground. If your men are telling you otherwise—they're lying."

Yoji's eyes twitched for a moment, but he remained unmoved. "We each create our own reality," he said. "Time will tell." His voice was hollow, and I could tell he didn't really believe Teddy was dead. I decided not to press it—I knew what coming to terms with the fact that someone you loved was gone was like. Hadn't I refused to believe that Ohiko was dead for weeks afterward, even though I had seen the ninja slay him right in front of me, held him in my arms while he breathed his last?

"The question is, how to proceed?" Yoji said. "You must convince your father that my people were not responsible for what happened at the wedding." Yoji's cigar had gone out, and when he lit another match, I saw that the skin

80

around his eyes was sagging and tired. In a flash, I understood that Yoji wanted to save the dying Yukemura empire.
He believed he didn't have very much longer to live, and he
wanted to ensure the continuation of his family before he
died. It was all written on his face, on the slope of his shoulders, in the careful, resigned way he relit his cigar.

"Why should I believe that?" I asked, shifting a little on
the couch, trying to push down the flood of memories that
threatened to overwhelm my ability to deal with the here
and now. "It was certainly your men who tried to kidnap
me. And your men who chased me down that night near
Vibe."

"Yes, I orchestrated the kidnapping. But we did not want
you harmed. We were eager for the wedding to take place
as planned. I'm sure Takeda explained to you about the
money, and—"

"But what about the thugs who attacked me on the subway platform? Or the ones who followed me to Vegas and
tried to kill me there?" I interrupted, forgetting myself for a
moment. "You admitted you've been following me this
whole time. And Teddy told me you were angry with him for
failing in his duties."

Yoji shifted nervously in his seat and sat up, seeming to
engage in the conversation fully for the first time. "That
wasn't me," Yoji said emphatically. "I heard about those
attacks from my men. If you hadn't been able to take care of
yourself, they would have intervened. As it was, I believe

Takeda got rid of the ninja who attacked you in Las Vegas. And as for Takeda—he *was* a disappointment." Yoji sighed. "But is it not a father's lot to be disappointed in his son?"

I gazed at him, and he looked back at me, his eyes clear and unblinking. I believed he was telling the truth.

"So who were they?" I asked.

Yoji shrugged. "I don't know. If our families were joined, we could find them and crush them."

"But don't you see?" I asked. "If you help me find out who's responsible for trying to destroy the Kogos, my father will have no choice but to agree to a union between our families. Honor will require it. You will have done him a great service." Yoji sat quietly, his tired face unmoved. "And besides," I continued, speaking quickly now, afraid that if I stopped talking, Yoji would tell us to leave, "I know you want to know who killed Teddy. And I believe that the people who killed him are the same people who put my father in a coma and murdered my brother."

Yoji turned the long box of cigar matches over and over in his hand. The jostling matchsticks clicked rhythmically with every turn, sounding unnaturally loud in the oppressive silence of the suite.

"Don't you want justice for Teddy?" I pleaded, refusing to give up. More than ever, I realized that Hiro and I were going to need Yoji's resources (and protection) if we wanted to end this thing once and for all.

"What's done is done," Yoji said, shifting slightly in his

wingback chair. "As I've said, if your father will agree to a union between the families, then I'm sure all this will be taken care of in time. If I were you, I would return to Japan and seek the protection of your family." Yoji puffed on his cigar. I watched his shadowed face closely, and it was then that I knew—Yoji was actually *scared* of whoever it was that wanted me dead. I instinctively looked over at Hiro, wondering if he sensed it, too, but his face was blank. Goose bumps came out on my skin. If Yoji *Yukemura* was too terrified to confront these people, then how could there be any hope for Hiro and me?

"My father's in a coma," I whispered. "You know there's nothing I can do."

"Someone will soon be appointed head of the family if he doesn't awaken," Yoji said, impatience creeping into his voice. "But we can hope for the best."

The fear and distrust in the room were becoming stifling. Something had been released into the air, and I didn't have the strength to argue with Yoji anymore. I rose to leave.

"Thank you for your time," I said. I heard Hiro rise and then felt the warm weight of his hand on my shoulder as he followed me to the door.

"Little Hiro Uyemoto, I see that you've become a man," Yoji called after us. I stopped in my tracks. How did he know Hiro's name? I looked at Hiro, whose hand slipped slowly from my shoulder. A muscle worked in his jaw.

"Your father works for me now," Yoji said, his voice still tired but suddenly a bit more menacing. I had a feeling that *this* was the Yoji Yukemura whose name inspired fear in the streets of Tokyo and L.A., the man Shigeto pictured as he sat in his self-made prison. "Did you know that?" Yoji asked.

I gasped. Hiro said nothing and reached for the doorknob.

"Yes, he'd fallen on hard times—but he's an invaluable addition to our organization. I'm sure he'd be pleasantly surprised if his son followed suit. What do you say, Hiro? How about coming to work for the Yukemuras? Then you can put this ridiculous American vacation behind you. It's time to grow up, don't you think?"

Hiro slowly lowered his hand from the doorknob. I stared at his face, searching desperately for answers. Was this really happening? Hiro, my ideal of honor and all that was right—was he, too, tainted by the yakuza's long reach? *You lied to me,* I thought with dawning horror.

"If it's our feud with the Kogos you're worried about," Yoji pressed on, "then clearly this conversation should assure you that we want nothing more than an end to that unpleasantness. If you do well for our family, we will adopt you as our own—and perhaps the families can be joined through you and Heaven."

My head was spinning. I reached out to a nearby table for support and resisted the urge to look at Hiro. I was scared of what I might read on his face. Cigar smoke hung in the air, and the room seemed to revolve, as though I were looking at it from the back of a merry-go-round horse. *This isn't happening,* chanted a voice in my head. *Not happening, not happening.*

Yoji stood up. "I know you've been living a life of poverty here in the U.S. Such self-denial is unnecessary. If you come work for me, you will have everything you desire. And I'll be more than happy to allow you to train your own men. From what I understand, you've worked miracles with Heaven." Yoji took a step forward. I forced myself to look at Hiro. Why was he listening to this? Was he actually considering Yoji's offer? "So," Yoji wheedled, "will you join us?"

The room was silent.

"No," Hiro said, and opened the door. Joe and Stevenson appeared instantly to block the way.

"Everything all right, sir?" Joe asked.

"Let them go," Yoji said. "Hiro, my offer still stands." Yoji turned to look at me. "If you care about your friend here, then you'll convince him to join us. Anything less would be suicide." Yoji's voice was threatening.

Hiro strode out of the room, pushing past the bodyguards. After a moment I followed him. His walk was stilted and awkward, nothing like Hiro's graceful, loping stride.

I felt like I was following a stranger.

As soon as the door shuts behind them, the memories rush in. Staring out at the glowing pool I'll never swim in, I feel transported to the time when my Takeda was a child and he and Hiro used to play together. They were very young . . . I doubt if either of them remembers it. Back then, Konishi used to keep his precious son, Ohiko, away from the other children, as if he were too good to mix with the likes of us. That was before the Yukemuras gained the power they had sought, before the feud started with an unfortunate killing of one of Konishi's top men. A poor decision—one made by my father just before he died and one that changed the course of my whole life.

But Hiro has turned into the kind of man I always hoped Takeda would become: thoughtful, serious, committed. None of that hip-hop gangster nonsense, none of the dabbling in drugs and parties that clouded Takeda's every decision, not to mention his sense of duty and honor. Unfortunately, Hiro has the same self-righteous streak his father used to have—before I broke him. I wonder if the boy realizes that his father would never have come to work for me if Hiro hadn't left. That was what finished him. When Hiro turned his back on his family, there was nothing to prevent his father from fully embracing the yakuza lifestyle he'd flirted with throughout his career. When a man's son turns against him, what is left for him to strive for?

I often wonder that myself. Takeda, for all his flaws, was my son. Is my son. I believe that he lives. I will not accept his death. But his short life has been a waste thus far, and now I keep asking myself what I could have done differently. His mother spoiled him, but she is not to blame. He was our only child. I should have put my foot down, been more strict, but he was the child of our old age and I loved him. He arrived long after we had given up hope of being able to have a child. And now he's gone.

Where are you now, my little Takeda? I will find you eventually. If not in this life, then in the next.

Heaven Kogo is a brave girl. Much like her father. She would have been a perfect wife for Takeda, not one of these useless society mannequins but a woman who could think and reason and keep him in line. Nothing like that awful stepmother of hers—cold, caring only for the next season's fashions, difficult to converse with. I always wondered why Konishi married that Mieko when he could have had his pick of any woman in Japan. The rumor was that he had a mistress who he continued to see after his marriage. I wouldn't be surprised. Many of us did.

But these are thoughts whose time has passed. The river of time has flowed on, and one never fishes in the same waters twice.

I am too old to risk much more. Once I had courage and passion. Now I am afraid.

I hope Heaven finds the answers she is looking for. But

something tells me that this journey is coming to an end—
for all of us.

I'll remain here until the morning light filters in through
the trees. Only then will sleep come to me.

Yoji

7

"Heaven," Hiro said as soon as we got into the car, "I—"

"No," I snapped, glancing at the man I had thought I knew so well. "Shut up. I need to think for a second." Hiro pressed his lips together and he blinked twice, then nodded, giving me my space. I slid into the passenger seat and leaned back against the headrest, covering my eyes with my hands. The last few days had caught up to me all at once and I felt empty inside. I wanted to curl into a ball and forget all I had seen and felt, starting with the attack in our hotel room in Tijuana. The web of emotions I was navigating, the confrontations with Shigeto, Karen, Yoji—it was all too much. And now this.

"How could you have lied to me about this?" I blurted, uncovering my eyes and turning to face Hiro. Even with everything that had happened, I couldn't help but admire the clean line of his profile as he navigated the car out of the lot. I doubted everything I had heard up in Yoji's suite. It would have been so much easier not to believe it.

"I can explain, Heaven," Hiro said softly. "Let's just go get some food and talk about it."

"Fine," I said. I was starving anyway. I stared out the window and watched the streets go from chic to run-down and seedy as Hiro drove back toward Hollywood. The question that bothered me the most was this: If I was so good at reading people, then how was it that I'd never once suspected that Hiro himself was connected to the yakuza? And once that question was out there, a million more followed. What else was I missing? Why hadn't he just *told* me? It would only have drawn us closer.

I rubbed my eyes. Without some sleep, it wasn't likely I'd come to any conclusions. I only hoped what Hiro had to say would make sense.

Hiro pulled into the parking lot of 'Round the Clock, the same fifties-themed diner he'd taken me to way back when we'd first met. That day, I remembered, my crush on him had just been starting to blossom, and so slowly that I wasn't entirely aware of it myself. Now we were a couple and we were going there to fight. It would have been almost typical if our situation hadn't been so bizarre.

I ignored Hiro while I read the menu and ordered a cheeseburger with cheese fries and a cherry Coke. I resisted ordering a slice of pie on the spot just to piss him off.

Hiro got the veggie burger and I wanted to kick him. He wasn't even a vegetarian. Couldn't he give the whole healthy-living thing a rest? I'd seen him eat a cheeseburger before.

Hiro cleared his throat. "What Yoji said was true," he said, and reached for my hand. I pulled it away.

"Do you have a quarter for the jukebox?" I asked. I wasn't going to make it easy, no way. He'd have to fight for this one.

Hiro sighed and pulled some change out of his pocket. "Can I continue?" he said, keeping his hands to himself this time.

"Whatever you want," I said, pretending to read through the song catalog on the minijukebox at our table but not really seeing anything at all. My heart was pounding so loud, I felt like Hiro must have been able to hear it.

"I never explained to you fully why I decided to leave Japan. A large part of it was my father's yakuza connection."

"And when you found out the Yukemuras had tried to kidnap me, you never thought it might be nice to let me know your father was on their side?" I snapped, punching random numbers into the jukebox.

"Believe me when I tell you that I had no idea my father was a member of the yakuza." Hiro paused. "He wasn't when I left home," he added softly.

"I'm supposed to believe that?" I turned to look at him, and my cold facade almost crumbled. He looked so tired

91

and defeated. I'd never seen Hiro with less life in him.

"I hope you will." Hiro clammed up as the waitress, wearing the diner's signature little pink shift, set down our plates. I immediately drowned my cheese fries with ketchup and started shoving them in my mouth. I didn't feel hungry anymore, but I didn't want Hiro to know how upset I was. Better to be angry.

"My father was a legitimate businessman for most of my childhood," Hiro said. "Just as you never realized that your father was involved with the yakuza—that he was the oyabun, the boss, even—I had no idea at all when the switch occurred." Hiro took a deep breath. "Now you know that the yakuza's fingers extend to every section of business in Japan. My father owned several very profitable lumber companies. His father, my grandfather, profited greatly during the reconstruction after World War II. That's where the Uyemoto fortune came from." Hiro paused and toyed with his veggie burger.

I stopped eating. It had never occurred to me to ask how Hiro's family had made their money when I met him. That's how naive I'd been when I'd first arrived here—

I'd never questioned how my own father became rich—or how anyone else had. These were just the people I'd grown up around, and in that world, everyone had money.

Hiro looked out at the parking lot, his eyes gazing far away somewhere, back to the Tokyo of his childhood. "What I didn't know was that payouts to the yakuza were the norm. All my grandfather's life, and my father's life, they'd always given a generous cut to the local gangs. It wasn't a choice—it was the cost of doing business."

"That's horrible," I whispered.

"Yes, it's awful, isn't it? Even worse when you realize that the yakuza consider themselves modern-day samurai. That's why Ohiko and I were raised with the kind of training we were—but I'm getting ahead of myself."

"Go on," I said.

Hiro took a sip of his iced tea. "After my grandfather died, my father decided he wanted to expand the business even more. When I was just starting secondary school, he made a bad decision that changed everything." Hiro's eyes met mine. "He took a loan from the Yukemuras' saiko-komon."

"Who was that?" I asked, recognizing the term for senior adviser.

"His name was Tetsuo Nakanishi, not that it matters. He's dead now. Killed by another family, undoubtedly. I was never told which one. And I never asked."

I pushed my plate away.

"The interest rates, of course, were brutally high. But my father thought he had a foolproof plan for getting the money back. It was hundreds of millions of yen, though, and things didn't go as planned. Eventually my father had to admit he couldn't pay. They threatened to kill him and to kill my mother and me if he didn't agree to let the

93

S
A
M
U
R
A
I

G
I
R
L

Yukemuras use his business as a cover for their operations."

"Like what?" I asked.

"Gun running, drugs—pretty much anything illegal you can imagine. My family had been in business so long that they could import almost anything without much trouble."

"I see," I said.

"My father thought it was his only hope. So he said yes."

"But Yoji said that your father had 'finally' begun working for him," I said, confused. "It sounds like you knew he was working for Yoji all along."

"In a sense, yes," Hiro answered, motioning to the waitress for some more water, "but my father dealt mainly with this Nakanishi character—and with the man who took over as saiko-komon after he died. My father refused to become an official member of the family with an official title, and the Yukemuras didn't care, as long as their shipments continued to make it in safely. It was only later that Yoji began to pester my father about becoming a shingiin or something like that."

"A counselor?" I said. "But why? Why would Yoji care?"

"Because then my father would be bound to him by a blood oath." Hiro stared down at his plate.

"Please eat something," I said, and touched his hand lightly. My anger had morphed into sadness. Hiro picked up his sandwich and took a bite. The waitress refilled

94

our glasses with water and he drank his down in one go.

"So when did you know that all this had happened?"

"My father called me into his office one day when I was eighteen. He told me everything. Obviously I was the one who was going to take over the business, and he wanted me to know what I was in for. He explained that dealing with the yakuza was all about survival but that it *was* possible to keep on their good side without taking that blood oath."

"But you didn't believe him?"

"I was young," Hiro said. "But I wasn't stupid. I was starting to suspect certain things before that conversation with my father, and I had already learned to loathe the yakuza for the way they twisted the bushido to their own ends. The Way of the Warrior is a sacred tradition, and it seemed to me that my father's reasoning was deeply flawed."

"So you ran away . . . ," I murmured.

"Not just then. First I went to Kyoto to study in a dojo there and to meditate upon what I should do. The answer came to me that I should leave my family and start a new life here in the U.S., where I might be able to teach others, eventually, about the samurai way of life. To bring it back to its pure state, but in a way applicable to modern living."

"I can't believe you never told me any of this." I shook my head. "It just boggles my mind that you could keep such a huge chunk of your life hidden from me."

"Heaven, I am *so sorry*," Hiro said, grabbing my hand.

95

This time I let him. "You have to understand—I thought I'd left that part of my life behind forever, and I thought it had nothing to do with your situation. As far as I knew, my father was just someone who did occasional dirty work for the Yukemuras. . . . He's rich, yes, but I thought there was no way he'd know anything about the politics of the family."

"But didn't you think it would make me feel better? Do you know how guilty and . . . and . . . *dirty* I felt when I finally found out that my father was the Kogo oyabun?"

"I can only say I'm sorry again and again until you believe me, Heaven," Hiro pleaded, his voice husky as he squeezed my hand. "It was a stupid decision. I see that now. At the time I just—I thought that it might minimize what you were going through. Can you understand that? I didn't want *your* problems to be clouded by *my* problems."

"But *why* couldn't you have told me later?" I said, tears filling my eyes. "I loved you so much and you know I would have understood." Hiro's eyes glistened. I pulled my hand away and reached for a napkin.

"I would have told you, Heaven. I know that's probably hard for you to believe right now, but it's the truth. You have to admit, there hasn't been much time for sharing confidences since things . . . changed between us."

"I guess," I said doubtfully, trying to staunch the tears that kept welling up and sliding down my nose. Why did I have to be such a baby?

"Can you please forgive me, Heaven?" Hiro begged,

touching my knee softly under the table. Part of me wanted to just say, *Okay, forget it, let's move on.* To get back the cozy feeling I was experiencing for the first time, the feeling of having someone around who cared about me *the most.* But another, deeper, more tentative voice inside me warned: *You can forgive him now, but it will never be the same. How can you trust someone who doesn't tell you the truth? Who has so many secrets?*

I moved my knee away. "I don't know," I whispered.

"Please," he said, his voice strained with emotion. It didn't take any extra perception to feel the tension in the air between us. You could have cut it with my katana. I stared blearily at my cheese fries through the fog of my tears.

"Heaven? Oh my God! Is that really you?" A cheery voice rang out, shocking me out of the moment and back into the booth in the crowded diner. I looked up.

Cheryl—she was alive!

8

"Cheryl!" I shrieked, jumping out of the booth. Cheryl style, she had yelled out to me from across the diner, and now she shimmied between the tables toward us, waving her hands and ignoring the irritated grumbles of the customers whose heads she was bashing with her oversized handbag.

"Heaven Kogo, you crazy girl!" Cheryl pushed between the last set of tables and threw herself into my arms. We did a little dance right there in the middle of the diner. Tears were streaming down my cheeks—one part runoff from my conversation with Hiro, one part relief—I hadn't known whether Cheryl had made it out of the fire alive, and the thought that she might not have had been too much to confront. I'd been in total denial about what had happened. Only when I saw her did I realize what I'd been repressing since I'd fled L.A. for Vegas.

"Look at you," I said, holding her away from me. "I just—I can't believe you're okay!"

"I'm *fine*," Cheryl said. "Wait a minute—" She grabbed me by the shoulders and spun me around.

"What?" I said, wiping my eyes.

"I *love* your hair! I can't believe you finally cut it!"

"Hiro did it," I said, laughing. Cheryl looked over at Hiro, who had been standing next to the booth, waiting for us to finish our hellos.

"Hiro!" Cheryl squealed. "You're a blond!" She grabbed his hands and pulled him toward her for a peck on each cheek. Hiro smiled at me over her shoulder, and I mustered a weak grin back. Cheryl showing up when she did had certainly diffused our confrontation.

"Sit down," Hiro said. "Tell us everything that happened."

"Scrootch," Cheryl commanded, pushing into the booth next to me. She grabbed a waitress by the apron and, ignoring her dirty look, ordered her favorite, French toast. It had been less than a week since I'd seen her, but she'd changed her hair. Instead of being pink-streaked, it was now a bright, Manic Panic red. Her face looked a little skinny, as if she hadn't been eating enough, but she certainly had the same old energy as ever. The only thing different about her was her clothes—they were still funky, but they covered a lot more than usual, which was weird, because it had been so hot lately.

"How's your ankle?" Hiro asked. She had hurt it during the attack in the subway right before the fire.

"It's totally fine," Cheryl chirped. "It was just a mild sprain. A few days in bed and it was back to normal. Still a little swollen, but it doesn't hurt."

"But what *happened*?" I asked, drinking in her presence. "Were you already in the house when the fire started?"

Cheryl's smile wobbled for a second, but soon she was grinning again. "I was there. The taxi dropped me off and I went inside. I crashed out on the couch, like, immediately. That whole Marcus thing just threw me for a loop, you know?"

I nodded sympathetically. Marcus was a guy Cheryl had started dating at Vibe, and we'd all found out that night that he'd been using her just to get to me. He and his henchmen had almost killed us both.

"I don't think it was that much later—I woke up and the whole living room was filled with smoke. I tried to get out the front door, but the flames blocked me. So I ran into the bathroom. Well, hopped."

"Oh, Cheryl," I said. "I'm so sorry."

"You should be," she snapped, surprising me. Then, "Just kidding," she added, giggling.

"Cheryl, don't do that!" I squealed. "You totally freaked me out."

Cheryl squeezed my hand. "Come on, Heaven—if it

hadn't been for you and Hiro, Marcus and his bangers would have thrown me in front of the Metro train. You're so gullible."

"But if it hadn't been for me—" I started.

"Whatever," Cheryl said, waving my apologies away. "Listen to my story. It's just getting good!"

"Okay," I said, and glanced at Hiro, who was still smiling a little bit. *His sense of humor is developing nicely, at least,* I thought. He seemed to get a kick out of Cheryl's colorful, nonstop storytelling.

"So all the time I was hopping toward the bathroom," Cheryl continued, the bangles on her wrist jangling with each gesture, "all I could think was 'stop, drop, and roll.' You know, like they used to teach in school? But that didn't seem to make any sense—then I remembered I wasn't on fire yet, so it wouldn't really help. So I finally got into the can, grabbed my bathrobe, and soaked it with water."

"Good thinking," Hiro said.

"Thanks! Anyway, I threw that over me and crawled down the hall to the bedroom, then sort of dropped out the window into the bushes."

"Were the fire trucks already there?" I asked.

"Yeah. But I didn't stick around. I went over to a friend's house. I just thought it might not be the best thing if people started asking questions, you know? I mean, I thought you guys might have been ambushed or something!"

"No—we came home after picking up my bag from Vibe,

and that's when we saw that the house was on fire. The whole place was surrounded by police and firemen, so we figured they had it under control." I ruffled Cheryl's hair. "I'm so glad you're okay!" I said, feeling the tears pricking behind my eyes again. "I don't know what I would have done if you'd been hurt . . . or . . ."

"Cut it out, you," Cheryl said. "You're going to make me cry and it's going to screw up my makeup."

"But you lost everything . . . ," I said, guilt washing over me.

"Don't worry about *that*," Cheryl said, grinning. "It was all crap anyway. What happened next was the crazy part!"

Cheryl's French toast arrived, and when I smelled it, my appetite came back with a vengeance. I took a big bite of my cheeseburger.

"Can I have a fry?" Cheryl said, grabbing one off my plate. She dunked it into the puddle of syrup around her French toast. "Mmm, gooey," she purred. "So where have you guys been? Where did you go after you saw the fire?"

"But wait—what happened next?" I asked.

"Later," Cheryl said. "Come on, I'm dying to know where you guys have been."

"I put Heaven on a bus for Vegas," Hiro said.

"No way!" Cheryl yelped. "That's so awesome. Did you, like, go undercover?"

"Kind of . . . ," I said. I studied Cheryl's face as she picked at her meal. Something was a bit different about her—a hardness around the mouth? A frantic look in the eye? The signs weren't adding up to anything I could understand. She was the same old Cheryl, but like Cheryl times ten. I wondered if she was on something.

"So? Spit it out," Cheryl prodded.

I decided it was best to tell her everything that had happened. There was no reason not to, really. It might be dangerous for her to be seen with us, but there was nothing I could tell her about my "Vegas vacation" that the people who were out to get us didn't know already. For the second time that night Hiro and I explained what had happened. Only this time Cheryl interrupted frequently. When I told her about how Hiro had come to Joshua Tree and we'd decided to start a new life together in Europe, she let out another high-pitched squeal.

"No way! You guys are totally going out now?"

I blushed. People at the booths around us were staring at Hiro and me as if they expected us to start making out right there.

"Cheryl . . . shhh . . . ," I said.

"Sorry," she hissed in a stage whisper only slightly quieter than her normal voice. "It's just—I can't believe it! It's so perfect!" Cheryl launched into an assessment of our relationship. It was so typical, I had to laugh.

"You are so *beyond*," I said. "After everything we've told you, *that's* all you can think about?"

Cheryl's face fell for the second time since she'd sat

down, but again she quickly recovered. "I'm sorry, you guys—everything you've had to go through just sucks so bad—I'm trying to look at the positive side of things."

"I know you are," I said.

"So now what?" Cheryl asked.

"Well," Hiro said, "we hadn't really discussed it. But we're probably going to get out of L.A. tomorrow morning. Drive back down to Las Vegas, maybe, and figure out our next step."

"It's too great!" Cheryl said. "You have to come stay in my kick-ass sublet."

Hiro looked taken aback. "You found a new place already?" he said, glancing at me. I'd been thinking exactly the same thing.

"Yeah—like I said, everything really turned out for the best." Cheryl's face fell. "Heaven," she said, turning to me and grabbing my hand. "There's something I have to tell you." Her eyes were wide, and she was chewing nervously on the nails of her free hand.

"What is it?" I asked gently, taking her hand again. Maybe she was about to tell me the thing I had sensed but couldn't name.

"Well, remember how I told you my family didn't have any money? And how I was always talking about how you needed to learn to fend for yourself?"

"I remember," I said. I'd felt so guilty when I couldn't make rent on our house. I knew Cheryl didn't get any support—financial or otherwise—from her family.

"Well . . ." Cheryl took a deep breath. Then, in a rush, "It was a lie. The whole thing. My family lives in Santa Cruz. My dad is an entertainment lawyer and my mother comes from money. *A lot* of money. It's true that I was supporting myself, but they've always given me plenty of cash whenever I needed it. They didn't exactly understand why I was living the way I was, but they accepted it. They just hoped I'd get tired of the working life and decide to go to college." Cheryl looked at me pleadingly. "I'm just so sorry I lied to you."

"Cheryl," I said, giving her a hug. "I totally understand. Believe me, I understand that it's hard letting people know you come from that kind of privilege."

"Really? You're not mad?"

I shook my head. "Nope. I just wish that you'd felt comfortable letting me in on your little secret."

Cheryl sighed. "Believe me, I wanted to. It's just—I'd gotten so used to it being a secret, know what I mean?"

I nodded. Boy, did I ever.

"So your parents sublet a place for you?" Hiro asked.

Cheryl wiped her eyes. "Kind of. It turned out that some good friends of theirs needed a house sitter for a few months. They went off to the south of France for the summer." Cheryl grinned. "The place rocks!"

"That's great!" I said. "So cool of your parents to let you stay in L.A. Where is it?"

"Studio City. Come on," Cheryl wheedled, totally back to her spastic self. She never could stay down for long. "You guys will *love* it. It's a duplex with four whole bedrooms, a pool in the building, health club—the works."

"You won't get in trouble for having guests, will you?" Hiro asked cautiously.

"In trouble? No way! The people I'm sitting for are, like, so mellow. As long as no one breaks their weird sculpture collection." Cheryl giggled. "It's not like I'm having a mad party or anything—I'm saving that for later."

"Well, if you're sure you don't mind . . . ," I said.

"Listen," Cheryl said. "It's just too easy. We'll go return your rental so you can at least not get as *totally* ripped off as you would if you kept it for another couple of days, and then you can take my car down to Vegas."

"What will *you* drive?" Hiro asked, running his hand through his hair.

"I've got a sporty little convertible that comes with the house. I'm driving it right now. See?" Cheryl pointed to the parking lot, where a gold BMW sat diagonally across two spots.

"Great parking job," I said, laughing.

"Hey—I'm just getting used to it! Besides, I thought I'd only be in here for a minute!"

"You are too much," I said.

"I know, I know," she said, dragging her handbag out from under the table. "Listen—you guys think about it while

I go to the bathroom. Here's some money for the check."

Cheryl threw a fifty down on the table and headed for the bathroom.

"I'm so happy for Cheryl," I said, looking at Hiro. I was glad we had something else to talk about besides what I'd learned earlier at Yoji's.

"Yes," Hiro answered. "But don't you think she's acting a little . . ." He paused, searching for the word. "Hyper?"

"Well, she *was* talking a mile a minute," I said, glancing around to make sure Cheryl wasn't behind me.

"And did you notice how glassy her eyes were?"

"Yes. And she only ate about two bites of her food," I added, staring at her plate of drooping French toast. "I think it might be drugs."

Hiro frowned. "That's not good."

"I know," I said. "But she's been through a lot. Maybe we're just reading too much into her behavior." I wasn't about to tell Hiro that, knowing the way Cheryl could drink, I wouldn't exactly have been shocked if she'd moved on to some other substance.

"Well, you know her better than I do . . . ," Hiro said.

I sighed. I felt like I was always being critical of Cheryl's behavior . . . which was pretty lame of me, considering how generous Cheryl had always been.

"You know what?" I said. "I think we should go. After all, where else are we going to stay tonight? And as for borrowing her car—it's probably a good idea."

107

"You're right," Hiro said. "No doubt they've got the license number of the rental down by heart at this point. And it's only one night."

"Fine," I answered. "We'll do it." I was tired from the effort of noticing every little thing that went on around me, and the cheeseburger had made me want to curl up right there in the booth and pass out. One thing I knew was that since the night of the wedding, it had always been Cheryl who'd helped me out of tight spots. And she'd almost gotten killed doing it. Plus she'd never lied to me. Not like *some* people. I studied Hiro's face.

"Heaven," he said, his voice soft.

"No," I said. "I'm not ready yet." I slid out of the booth and stretched. Just for tonight, I was going to relax. Tomorrow would come soon enough.

Besides, I was psyched to see Cheryl's phat pad.

I knew Heaven wasn't dead. Why should she be? I was the one who got stuck in the house, who got sent back there alone even though I'd screwed up my ankle and had no idea what the hell was going on.

Damn, this bathroom is cold! Would it kill them to turn down the air-conditioning a little bit? I mean, come on, just because it's hot out doesn't mean it has to be subzero in here. My ass is freezing. For once I'm almost glad I'm wearing long pants.

Deep breath. Inhale. There. Just a few bumps until we get back to the apartment and Heaven and her boy toy settle in. Then I can indulge as I please. Wipe the nose, wait for that bitter trickle down the back of my throat. There. I saw Heaven giving me that "mom" look earlier. She probably can't help it, but it's a little disappointing she didn't learn how to loosen up a bit more when she was working at Vibe. I think she suspects I might be "indulging" a little. But she won't say anything, I think. Not in the next few hours, anyway, and that's all that matters. Oh God, the thought of some kind of "intervention" from her makes me feel nauseated. Miss Good Girl. A lecture is exactly what I don't need—*especially from her.*

After tonight I'll give up the coke for good anyway. Get my hands on some of the real good stuff for the pain. Some of those high-grade pharmaceuticals. Because it hurts. The doctors said the burns would heal soon, that they were deep but small enough not to have to worry too much about. Just a bit of scarring. I'll have to go see a specialist about that.

Freaking fantastic. One day I'm out with the hottest guy I've ever dated, the next minute I'm elephant girl, forced to dress in some wack Eileen Fisher ensemble like a forty-year-old hippie from Marin.

Another bump. Aaah, that's good. It makes everything so much easier. The planning, the talking. Getting through the night.

When Heaven and Hiro are gone, I'm packing my bags and moving out. Up to Santa Cruz, maybe, or even Big Sur. I've got the funds, and soon I'll have even more cash, so why not live a little? I'll come back in a few months when everything blows over—open my own shop, maybe. Or how about New York City? That might be the place for me. Forget this California bullshit. I could rent a place on the lower East Side with all the dough, hang at the cool clubs, get known on the scene.

My face looks a little pale in the bathroom mirror. I splash some water on it, make sure there's no blow left on my nose. Deep sniff. Good. My teeth are numb, love that. Spike up the hair. Not sure how I feel about this red, but it's kind of growing on me. Clothes—disaster, as previously mentioned. Now that I think about it, the look is a little Beyond Thunderdome. Oh, well, I'll buy new threads soon. Just have to bide my time.

Heaven's hair looks great, of course. She'd look good

bald and wearing a paper bag. Some people are just lucky. They have everything handed to them on a plate. She'll be fine. Nothing's going to happen to her.

They promised me that.

Cheryl

9

We cruised into the underground parking lot in Cheryl's building, tires squealing as she veered into a parking space marked Reserved. Cheryl drove like she did just about everything else—fast and with very little thought. Hiro let out his breath and relaxed his death grip on the arm of the car door. Attacks by ninjas? No problem. But put someone else at the wheel and it drove Hiro crazy.

The elevator from the parking garage opened directly into Cheryl's sublet.

"Wow," I breathed as I stepped into a space that looked like it had been ripped directly from the pages of *Architectural Digest*. "This is amazing."

Directly in front of us, a brushed metal circular staircase wound its way up to the second level. One wall of the apartment was all glass, and we could see outside to where a balcony looked out at the lights of the city. Dotted around the room was a series of abstract sculptures, all forged out of a dark, heavy metal—at first they looked like human figures, but when I got up close, I could see they were more like birds or animals. A few modernist leather sofas and chairs sat in the larger room in front of a huge fireplace. The effect was cold but stunning.

"Beautiful," Hiro said appreciatively.

"Isn't it *awesome*?" Cheryl threw her keys on a glass coffee table that wound around itself in a spiral shape. Very avant-garde. "This is one of four or five properties the Reeses—that's their name—have. A house in the south of France, something in London, I think, and New York City." Cheryl walked into the kitchen, a study in modern decor, and opened the Sub-Zero fridge.

"Whiskey? Or how about a beer?"

"No, thanks," I said. "I'm feeling a little tired."

"Hiro?" Cheryl asked, dumping ice cubes into a glass and walking over to the bar that lined the other side of the room, which was stocked with top-shelf liquor.

"No, thank you."

"Guess I'm drinking alone, then, ha ha." Cheryl poured whiskey over the ice cubes. She toasted us, then took a gulp.

"I'm sorry," I said. "It's just that it's been a really long day." It was as if Cheryl hadn't even heard any of the stuff we'd told her earlier, like she just wanted to forget it all and party down.

"Sorry? Don't be sorry," Cheryl said, leaning against the bar. "You guys probably just want to crash, huh? I mean, *I* would certainly want to hit the hay if I were you. But I can show you around if you want."

"Cool," I said, not wanting Cheryl to think we were just using her for a crash pad. I was still feeling pretty sensitive about that.

Cheryl knelt down by the fireplace and lit a match, and in just one second a fire was burning in the grate. "Gas fire," she explained. "Totally idiotproof." Cheryl lit a cigarette and threw herself onto the leather sofa. "Go grab yourself a soda or something and we can relax."

"I'll get us some water," Hiro said, stepping back into the kitchen. I sat down next to Cheryl on the couch.

"You smoke now?" I asked, then instantly regretted it. I hadn't meant to nag.

"Oh, I'm not really a smoker," Cheryl said, puffing happily on her butt. "You know, not like those old ladies you see who always have a cigarette jammed between their lips from first thing in the morning until last thing at night. The ones who fall asleep smoking and light their houses on fire."

I nodded. Cheryl was definitely on something. Her eyes darted back and forth, and it was almost as if her brain was programming words down to her mouth without any thought involved. She just couldn't stop talking.

"No, just here and there," she continued. "I'm tellin' ya,

it's been kinda harsh this last week, you know? I mean, the Marcus thing and the fire. I need to totally relax and chill and figure out what to do next." Cheryl sipped her whiskey. "So this just helps a bit," she said, gesturing vaguely toward her drink and her smoke. "For now."

"I understand," I said. While she talked, describing the details of the apartment, how four people could fit in the bathtubs, how the showers had "rain shower" heads, and how the curving staircase had been designed by a French architect named Baptiste, I only half listened to what was coming out of her mouth, turning my attention instead to the sound of her voice, the way her body moved. She gestured jerkily with her hands, and her lips were dry and cracked. All the signs only added up to what I already knew—she was doing drugs. It was as simple as that. I hoped her parents would check in on her once in a while, because there was no way I could confront her about this right now.

Cheryl jumped up. "Come on, guys," she said, grabbing her keys. "You *have* to see the pool before bed. It's on the roof, and you get the greatest view of the city from up there."

Hiro and I followed Cheryl back to the elevator. She was right. The pool was magnificent. Fountains tinkled along its edges. Muted lights showed how clear and clean the water was and didn't detract at all from the view Cheryl had promised. The three of us leaned against the railing. A cool breeze was blowing in from the desert, and the city lay peacefully beneath us. It was easy to imagine a celebrity party up there—Hiro and me holding glasses of champagne and wandering along the sides of the pool, maybe taking a break on one of the stone benches that lined the rooftop, each one nestled in its own grove of hibiscus flowers. *"Doesn't Reese look precious tonight?"* I'd say. *"She and Ryan are really a lovely couple."*

"It's so peaceful," Hiro said wistfully. I was pretty sure his reverie didn't include a star-studded cocktail bash. Screw perception—I wished I could just pry open his head and read his brain.

"Doesn't it rule?" Cheryl said. "Much better than that dump we were staying at on Dawson Street, huh, Heaven?"

"I liked our place," I said. My father's house wasn't as high-tech and modern as this one (except for his office, of course), but it was beautiful in its classic Japanese way—and just as cold. My room had been an oasis in a house where everything was always in the right place, where the rooms were always clean and the heirlooms were never touched. Moving in with Cheryl had been a blast. I'd loved the clothes on the floor, magazines strewn around the living room, dirty dishes piled up in the sink—and lots of crappy TV whenever I wanted.

"It was cozy," I said. "I think that's why I liked it."

"Cozy?" Cheryl said, snorting a little. "That's one word for it, I guess. You could also say messy and cramped.

Hey, did I tell you there's maid service here? She comes twice a week, so I don't have to do a damn thing."

"Why couldn't the maid just look after the house while the owners are gone, do you think?" Hiro asked.

"Beats the hell out of me," she said, laughing. "They probably think she'll steal some of their precious weird art or something if no one's around to keep an eye on her."

Cheryl lit another cigarette with shaky hands. I remembered how she hadn't really eaten anything that night, and everything she'd been through, and how I'd let her go home by herself the night of the fire. She would never have done that to me. Suddenly I felt terribly guilty for harping on the whole drug thing. It was probably just a phase—she'd snap out of it.

"Who wouldn't want their very own bird-man-camel sculpture?" I joked, and threw my arm around Cheryl. She stiffened under my touch, and I drew away. Her eyes had hardened, and the air between us suddenly felt sticky with a new emotion—the set of her mouth looked angry. "I think it's bedtime for us," I said, trying to smooth over the moment. Maybe the dope or whatever was making her paranoid.

Cheryl stubbed out her cigarette, and her face relaxed. "Shit. I'm sorry. You guys must be totally beat. Let's go back downstairs."

Back in the apartment, Cheryl took us up the staircase

to the second level. Rooms radiated off a central space with an arched ceiling—sort of a honeycomb effect. After showing us the master suite, where she was staying (bedroom, sitting room, walk-in closet, dressing room, sauna—the works), Cheryl led us to our bedroom.

"Here we go, the honeymoon suite," Cheryl joked. "This should be just about perfect for you guys." Cheryl winked at me and my face grew hot. The room had a huge king-size bed in it. There was a square, cream-colored armchair in the corner with a small table next to it and a floor lamp, and that was it. Two large abstract oils painted in camouflage colors hung above the bed. I avoided looking at Hiro. I'd much rather have had my own room, but I didn't feel like explaining anything to Cheryl. In fact, I was finding it draining having Cheryl around at all.

"Night, kids," Cheryl said with another wink after throwing some towels on the bed. The door clicked shut, and Hiro dropped his duffel on the floor, then sat on the bed.

"Heaven, about earlier—"

"I can't," I said harshly. Hiro lay still, his hand over his eyes. I reached out and pulled his hand away. He turned to look at me. "I'm sorry," I said, "but I think we should just sleep."

"Okay," he said, and kissed the palm of my hand. He rolled over and scooted under the covers. "Good night," I whispered, but he was already asleep. I'd forgotten that he hadn't had the benefit of a nap in the car that morning. Had it really only been this morning that we'd been in San Diego?

My eyes snapped open. I could hear breathing in the dark room, and my chest tightened with fear before I realized the breathing was my own. It came back to me in a rush: I was in Cheryl's sublet. Hiro was sleeping next to me, a warm body under the covers. I closed my eyes and tried to clear my mind. Best to go back to sleep. Who knew what the day would bring?

But sleep wouldn't come. In the night, with nothing to distract me, there was too much to remember. Teddy, Shigeto, Yoji—and the same strange feeling of "not rightness" I'd had ever since Cheryl had sat down with us in the diner. I rolled out of bed and stretched my legs. I was still in my gi pants and T-shirt, and my body felt stiff and unfamiliar. In the bathroom a small digital clock embedded in the wall flashed the time: 5:20. Soon it would be light. I splashed water on my face and examined my various bruises. No improvement there.

I decided to go downstairs and surprised myself by toying with the idea of bringing the Whisper along. No—that was idiotic. What would Cheryl say if she woke up to find me downstairs, a gigantic sword in my lap? Besides, looking for a glass of milk wouldn't be dangerous. I shook my caution away. Back on Dawson Street, Cheryl hadn't been exactly on top of keeping things like milk and eggs in the fridge, but with any luck the maid who came in twice a week was doing the shopping.

The apartment was still as I crept down the stairs, but a glow emanated from the living room. Cheryl hadn't turned off the fire. I tiptoed into the gleaming metal kitchen. Yes! A carton of milk was nestled in among the bottles of beer. I sniffed it. Seemed okay.

I took my glass of milk back to the sofa and sat down in front of the fireplace. Looking around the room, I realized what had been bothering me so much before—there was *nothing* in the apartment that said anything about the people who lived there. All you could tell was that they were rich and liked a modern look. No family photos, no little pieces of bric-a-brac. Even my father's house had pieces that clearly had been in the family for a long time. Everything in this living room looked like it had been bought all at once . . . but maybe that was what happened when you owned more than one place on more than one continent.

I ran my hands over the creamy leather of the couch. The furniture was much more expensive than I'd previously thought—well-made stuff, Italian. The kind of thing you had to special order. My stepmother, Mieko, had always had design books around, and I'd enjoyed flipping through them out by the pool. I sighed. That had been my life at one point—lessons in the morning, swimming laps in the afternoon, and drinking big glasses of iced green tea.

The fire started to feel too warm, so I wandered over to the inlaid marble table by the balcony doors. Cheryl's handbag was balanced precariously on the table's edge, and half the stuff inside was spilling out. I gently nudged the bag back to solid ground. A bunch of scrawled-on receipts, some pens. Tubes of Chap Stick and hand lotion. Before I could stop myself, I gingerly reached out and shifted the pile, curious about what else might be in there. Sticks of gum, a half-empty pack of Camels. I shook the bag a little bit, spilling out more of its contents. My heart was pounding.

A lighter. A compact. A pair of underwear. I had to smile—Cheryl had always said you should carry around an extra pair "just in case." It was all pretty much what I had expected. I flicked through the scraps of paper.

A thin pink slip caught my eye. At first I thought it was just another credit card receipt. I picked it up and squinted to read it in the firelight. Los Angeles National Bank. It was a deposit slip.

For twenty thousand dollars.

I read it again to be sure I had the amount right. Yep. Twenty grand. I dropped the slip on the table, my heart pounding harder now. I was willing to bet Cheryl's parents weren't in the habit of handing out twenty thousand dollars checks, especially when they'd already set her up with a place to live—rent-free. So who'd given her the money? I pushed part of the pile back into the handbag along with the deposit slip and grabbed Cheryl's car keys, shoving them into my pocket.

Suddenly I knew. Hiro and I had to get out of here. Now.

I dashed to the stairs. Halfway up I stopped. Footsteps. I froze. A door opened, then closed. A cough. Cheryl's.

I vaulted back down the stairs, using all my training to keep my footsteps soundless. In the living room I stared around me in dismay. Not only was it just starting to get light out, but the openness of the room meant that there was nowhere to hide. I couldn't let Cheryl know I was awake.

Her footsteps grew louder. In a minute she'd be downstairs. I leapt into the kitchen and searched for any kind of nook and cranny. I opened one of the lower cabinet doors to wedge myself inside, then noticed they all had glass doors set into the stainless steel frames. Not only would she see me, but she'd think I'd finally gone totally insane.

A beam. Without thinking, I shimmied up the beam and across the ceiling to the darkest part of the room, letting myself dangle horizontally from my arms and legs. *You're an idiot, Heaven*, said a voice in my head. *Like she's not going to notice you pulling a Spiderman up on the ceiling.* I prayed that she'd looked up at the twenty-foot ceilings enough times not to have to look up now. I concentrated on using my masking technique, shinobi-iri, and on keeping my breathing soft and even, in sync with the regular rhythms of the room, like the hum of the mammoth fridge.

I heard Cheryl's footsteps in the living room, and soon she was in the kitchen, carrying a cordless phone. She was wearing the same clothes she'd had on earlier, and from the looks of them, she'd never been to bed. She punched some numbers into the phone and then tucked it between her ear and neck. She opened the fridge and stared inside.

"They're here," she said, slamming the door of the fridge shut. I held my breath. Cheryl listened for a moment to a man's voice I could just barely hear on the other end of the line. "Karen called me from the dojo. I followed them from there."

Cheryl paused, listening. "All right," she said, "I'll be ready. You be ready with the rest of the money."

10

Cheryl clicked off the phone, and I heard her toss it onto the sofa. I started breathing again as I listened to her slide open the balcony door and slip outside. I strained my ears—it was just like being a big bat—and when I heard the hiss of a match, I knew she had stepped outside for a smoke. I slid down the beam and, masking myself in the shadows, crept as quickly as I could up to our bedroom.

"Hiro," I hissed, kneeling by his side of the bed.

His eyes snapped open. "What is it?" he said, instantly awake.

"It's a setup," I whispered fiercely. "I heard Cheryl talking to some guy on the phone—she said Karen called her from the dojo and she followed us from there."

"Do you have any idea who Cheryl was talking to?" Hiro

asked, sitting up and running his fingers through his hair, totally alert.

I shook my head.

"Let's get out of here," he said, pulling on his sneakers. "Cheryl can't stop us from leaving, but whoever she called might be able to."

I pawed through the duffel and grabbed the Whisper. Hiro shouldered the bag and we dashed down the stairs. Just as we reached the living room, Cheryl stepped inside from the balcony.

"Hey!" she shouted. "What are you guys doing?"

At the same moment the front door burst open and four men stepped into the room. Out of the corner of my eye I saw Cheryl scoot into the kitchen, out of harm's way. Hiro was already flying into the fight, arms spread.

One of the thugs hurtled toward me and I snapped around, pleased at the crunch my roundhouse kick made when it connected with his face. It was only when he went down that I saw he was one of the same guys who'd raided our hotel room in Mexico.

"You again," I gasped. A jolt of adrenaline flowed through my veins as I unsheathed the Whisper. These were the guys who'd killed Teddy—and they were going to have to pay.

One down. Hiro was holding off two others on the far side of the room. I prepared to engage thug number two— this guy was Japanese, and he knew his stuff. He was

125

carrying a bo—a long stick he wielded like a sword. He didn't just lumber toward me like the other guy had but skillfully herded me up against the counter, blocking my sword attacks with the bo. *Stupid, Heaven, stupid,* I said to myself. I knew better than to get backed against the wall. Block, punch, slice, block. Low block. My attacker kicked— dumb. We were too close for that. I grabbed his ankle and torqued it, using my counterweight to throw him off balance, then thwacked him with the side of my sword—I still couldn't bear the thought of impaling someone. He toppled, knocking over one of the metal statues. It only bought me a second, but it was enough time for me to push away from my tight spot. I vaulted over the counter and into the kitchen.

Cheryl sat cowering in the corner by the fridge.

"Why?" I yelled, watching the thug as he approached for more. Supporting myself between the countertops, I double kicked, driving him back. I jumped forward, and we engaged again, his bo crashing against my katana. If Hiro had had the sword, he would have been able to crack the bo in half with it—I just didn't have enough strength. I ducked and dodged, trying to find an opening for the blow that would finish him. "Why did you do this?" I repeated, screaming out my rage and frustration as I tried to hold off the thug.

"Because you almost got me killed, you bitch!" Cheryl shrieked. "Besides, how do I know anything you told me is even true? What if they're the ones telling the truth? You used me!"

Her words echoed in my head as I fought my way back out of the kitchen. Hiro had knocked out one of this attackers, who lay draped in front of the gas fire. Now the room was filled with the soft blue light of dawn, making it harder to use the shadows to slip around and surprise the goons. Mustering all my strength, I moved in for the kill, and with a grunt I swung the katana with all my strength at my opponent's arm, slicing through the skin. He moaned, then stumbled as the bo dropped from his hands. Then he came back for more. He was unstoppable, and my strength was flagging.

"Hiro!" I shouted, my words followed by a huge crash. Hiro had picked up one of the smaller sculptures and clocked his second guy over the head with it. *Crack* . . . the sound of his skull breaking was sickening, yet satisfying. I sensed Hiro jumping over the fallen thug as a mighty kick from my guy doubled me over and the katana went flying out of my hands. It was all I could do to block punch after punch—I was too worn down to get back on the offensive, and soon we were both fighting with my attacker. Hiro spun to the left, following the movement through with a thrust kick. The thug keeled over. Hiro felled him with a snap kick to the solar plexus. Boy, he was good.

"Let's go," Hiro said, grabbing my hand. I reached out and picked up the Whisper, wiping its blade quickly on the white throw rug, leaving a swath of dark red blood.

"You're just going to leave me here?" Cheryl called. "What if they do something to me?" she screamed, stumbling out of the kitchen. She looked so thin and pale, like a ghost—*No,* I corrected myself. *Like a worm.*

"You made your decision," Hiro said coldly, "and now you have to live with it."

"You're a liar!" I yelled. Cheryl recoiled as if I'd hit her. "Parents, my ass—I should have known you'd never live in some dump in Hollywood if you didn't have to. You're just a moneygrubbing—"

"Come on, Heaven," Hiro interrupted, gently tugging at my hand.

I pulled away. I was just getting started. "How could you do this?" I said, stepping toward Cheryl, who cringed away from me like a beaten dog. "Don't you know those people want to kill us? Do you understand that? This is not just some silly game!"

"They told me they wouldn't hurt you guys . . . ," Cheryl pleaded, twisting the fabric of her shirt.

"You disgust me," I spat out, and turned around.

"Screw you!" Cheryl wailed. "You left me to die in that house. And now I have to live with that for the rest of my life. Look at me. *Look* at me!"

I looked. With one swift movement Cheryl pulled her shirt off over her head and stood in front of us, wearing only a skimpy cotton bandeau.

Her skin was covered in ugly red blisters. Her arms had been badly burned, too, and the wounds were covered in Vaseline. They glistened. It wasn't as bad as it could have been, but it was pretty bad. *Well,* I thought, *that explains her new look, anyway.* I felt a twinge of guilt that I quickly shoved away. She'd almost gotten us killed.

"Do you see what you did to me? I'm going to be a *freak* for the rest of my life because of you!" Cheryl's eyes were wild. She was clearly losing it. "I can't even wear a regular *bra* because it hurts too much!"

"Heaven didn't set that fire," Hiro snapped. "The people you've been working for did."

"Let's just go, Hiro," I said. I looked at Cheryl one last time. "You're not worth any kind of explanation," I seethed. "You deserve whatever happens to you."

Hiro and I ran to the elevator. I punched the elevator button.

"No," Hiro shouted, "stairs."

We hurled ourselves out the front door into the stairway and took the stairs three at a time, jumping down to the landings as fast as we could.

"Now what?" Hiro gasped, about ten flights down. Only fifteen flights to go.

I fished Cheryl's car keys out of my pocket. "I'm on it."

We burst into the parking garage and I tossed Hiro the keys as we jumped into the BMW.

"Over there!" I yelled. We'd just been spotted by a group

of men wearing black suits and sunglasses. As two of them ran toward us, the others turned around and jumped into a black SUV. Hiro threw the BMW into reverse and we squealed out of the parking lot.

I reached over and grabbed Hiro's seat belt, pulling it across him and locking it in place. Then my own. Hiro jammed on the horn as we rocketed out of the parking garage without slowing down.

"To your right!" I yelled as a white minivan barreled toward us. Hiro swerved, and we narrowly avoided the car. Through the back windshield I could see the SUV gaining on us. "Go, go!" I screamed.

"I'm going!" Hiro sped though the streets of L.A., heading up into the Hollywood Hills. I braced my hands against the dashboard and prayed that whatever happened, we wouldn't hit too hard. Hiro veered off on side streets, taking the most circuitous path he could as the car climbed higher and higher up into the quiet streets of the Hills. We couldn't shake the SUV. With a jolt we spun onto Mulholland Drive, and soon we were taking the curvy twists at over seventy miles per hour. I squeezed my eyes shut.

"Hiro, stop it!" I said, my voice trembling. "This is too dangerous!" I peeked out my window and a wave of nausea passed over me as I saw how high up we were. "We're going to kill somebody if we don't die first!"

As if in answer to what I'd just said, I hear a loud screech and then a sickening crash from behind us. The SUV was driving in the wrong lane, and it had just forced a car into the wall of the canyon. At least it hadn't gone over the edge. I couldn't tell how bad the crash was because soon we'd cleared another bend and were climbing again.

"It'll be worse down in the city," Hiro yelled, both hands gripping the wheel, his face contorted with the effort of keeping control of the BMW. "Rush hour traffic's starting up."

"Please, Hiro," I pleaded.

Hiro didn't respond, but after a second he jammed the steering wheel to the left and peeled out into a turnaround. I held my breath as he inched the BMW into a ditch. With all the scrub, it was hard to tell where the road ended and the cliff began. I had to trust him.

The SUV sped past. After a minute Hiro backed the BMW out, and soon we were hurtling down into the city.

"I think we lost them," Hiro said after a few minutes. I closed my eyes for a moment, feeling the cool morning air whipping my hair around. "To Vegas, then?" Hiro said.

I nodded. I really didn't want to go back there, but it seemed like the best place to start.

"Heaven," Hiro began tentatively, "I want you to know that it was your heightened perception that saved us back there."

"That's a laugh," I said bitterly. "If I'd known what I was doing, we'd never have agreed to crash with Cheryl." I shook my head. "And that whole story about her parents? I totally bought it!"

"No—think about how amazing it is that you felt something in your sleep that you couldn't deny—that's what made you get up and check things out downstairs. If you hadn't"—Hiro exhaled slowly—"they could have killed us in our sleep."

"You would have woken up," I mumbled. It used to be that nothing made me as happy as a word of praise from Hiro. He was a strict trainer, and he rarely made much of small successes. But today his encouragement left me feeling flat. If my perception was so great, then why hadn't I picked up on Cheryl's deviousness from the moment I saw her at the diner? Or rather, why hadn't I listened to what my sixth sense had been trying to tell me all along? I'd just stupidly ignored the signs—the flashy car, the luxury pad, the strange way she was behaving. My skills must have been pretty shabby if they couldn't keep me from walking into a trap like that.

I looked over at Hiro, whose hands had finally relaxed on the wheel. He adjusted his mirror. *And what about Hiro's dirty little secret?* whispered a nagging voice in my head. *Shouldn't you have figured that one out for yourself, too?* It seemed like my perception wasn't very good at clueing me into things it knew I wouldn't want to believe.

"They're back!" Hiro yelled, breaking my reverie. I looked over my shoulder just in time to see the SUV bounding off a side street and skidding out behind us. It was so close, I could see the driver. He was Japanese, that much I knew, but I didn't recognize him. Hiro floored the gas.

We barreled down West Sunset, pushing our way toward Chinatown and the freeway. A blur of traffic zipped by us as Hiro ignored the stoplights and just kept on going. We had to get to the freeway.

Suddenly—sirens.

"Shit, shit, shit!" Hiro yelled as the police cruisers joined the chase.

"Go, go, go!" I yelled, finding it funny, even in the middle of such a terrible moment, that Hiro had allowed himself to swear—that was a first. But it wasn't funny for long. "There!" I shouted. The freeway entrance was just ahead. Hiro pushed the car to eighty-five, ninety, ninety-five miles an hour. He crossed two lanes of traffic and we were flying onto the ramp. And then . . .

Three cruisers pulled out in front of us, sirens wailing, blocking the entrance. Hiro slammed his foot on the brake, and my body lunged forward against the seat belt as the BMW spun around and ground to a halt. A fire bolt of pain coursed through my chest as the seat belt tightened across the same strip of chest torn up by yesterday's accident. I closed my eyes and tried to breathe through the hurt. Tears seeped out from under my eyelids.

Hiro clicked off his seat belt and put his arms around me. "Are you okay? What is it?" He put his hand on my face.

"Fine," I gasped. "It's just the seat belt." I loosened it,

sighing with release as the pain ebbed. "What happened to the SUV?" I murmured.

Hiro looked around. "Gone—they must have slipped away."

"Out of the car!" a disembodied voice boomed. The cops were screaming at us through a bullhorn. They'd exited their cruisers and were pointing their guns straight at us.

"I'm tired of running," I whispered, looking at Hiro. I'd never thought giving up would feel so good. But there was nowhere left to run to. I knew that now.

"Get *out* of the car with your hands *up*!" thundered the voice.

"We'd better get out," Hiro said.

I unlocked my door and stepped out of the BMW, hands raised above my head. Hiro did the same. Instantly the cops moved in and hurled us against the car's hood. Hiro and I looked into each other's eyes as they frisked us, then twisted our arms behind our backs and cuffed our hands.

"Is that your car?" the cop asked as she led me away. I ignored her, staring instead at Hiro, who was being led in another direction. I wondered how he'd feel if he knew I was ready to spill it all. The whole story.

"I said, *is that your car?*"

I wondered how it would feel being separated from him. I could tell he was trying to catch a glimpse of me, but the cops kept him moving forward.

The cop's hand tightened around my upper arm. "Listen, missy—"

"No," I said dreamily, "it's not mine."

The police shoved Hiro into the back of the cruiser. I slowed my steps, and the lady cop barked, "Get your ass moving!"

I watched the cruiser carrying Hiro pull away. His face appeared in the rear window, and as I watched, he mouthed the words, "I love you."

I looked away. There's really only one thing to say when someone tells you that.

And I knew I couldn't say it.

11

"How'd you guys score that Beamer back there?" the chubby cop asked through the grate separating the front and back seats of the cruiser. I ignored him.

"Yeah," the lady cop piped in, "did you rip that off in Beverly Hills or Pacific Heights or what?" They both cracked up. I closed my eyes and tried to be patient. The movies had also taught me that I didn't have to answer. "You have the right to remain silent. . . ." That was exactly what I planned to do, for now.

But I already knew I would tell them everything. I would tell *someone* everything, that is, but I wasn't going to waste my time blabbing to a couple of patrol cops. I watched the city float by in a darkened blur through the cruiser's tinted window. The time for taking stock of escape routes, for noticing the way the bars between the front and back seats of the cruiser were warped around the edges, for cataloguing every twitch and murmur of the cops up front, was over. My sense of perception stank. What I'd achieved with Shigeto was beginner's luck—any idiot could have seen the guy was terrified, drunk, a pushover. I'd bullied him. And then I'd failed where it really counted, missing both Cheryl's bitterness and Hiro's secrets.

"Almost there," Chubby Cop announced, and it sounded like his voice was coming from far away.

I should have known it was only a matter of time before they caught up to us—if the cops hadn't, the yakuza would have. Or somebody else. But who else? *Who?* All the facts I'd learned added up to create that one big question.

Maybe it didn't matter. I could see now what my life would be like if I kept running—lonely. Short. A continual series of missteps and failures. No, my only chance for survival was to spill the whole story. Let someone else deal with the fallout for a change.

We rolled up in front of the precinct, a squat building made of khaki-colored brick. I'd expected something a little more elaborate—Roman columns, statues, a soaring dome—but this looked more like the library a few blocks away from Hiro's house.

Inside was a different story—exactly what I'd expected from an L.A. police station. Chaos reigned. Some cops milled around drinking coffee and ignoring stacks of paperwork, while others led a steady stream of perps in handcuffs toward the reception area. A bum yelled at a cop, whose face grew redder as he tried to take the guy's prints. I wondered briefly what the bum had done, then craned my neck to stare at a seven-foot drag queen with the most cleavage I'd ever seen. I stopped and gawked as an officer dragged her toward the fingerprinting desk, but Chubby Cop passed me off to the lady cop and I quickly lost sight of Miss Thing.

Here I was just another criminal.

I caught a glimpse of Hiro being led away. The lady cop tugged me over to the front desk, where a female booking officer came out from around the counter and emptied my pockets.

"Name?" she asked.

"Heaven Kogo," I said, taking in my surroundings. It really *was* like in a movie. Maps of the city lined the walls, along with pictures of wanted criminals and missing children. I stared at them one by one—yep, there I was. It was the same picture they'd shown of me on the news a month or so after the wedding disaster. I still didn't know who'd leaked the fact that I was missing back then. My father had told me it wasn't him the last time I'd seen him.

The booking officer froze. "Say again?" she said.

"Heaven Kogo," I said patiently. "I'm up there on the wall."

"Hank," called out the booking officer to a cop seated at a desk just under the bulletin board where my picture hung. "Bring me that poster."

"Which one?" he yelled.

"Heaven Kogo," she said, eyeing me. Hank unpinned the flyer and brought it over.

"You changed your hair," Hank commented, staring at me, then back at the flyer. The picture had been taken about two years ago. It was incredible how much younger I looked. My hair was long, and sunglasses sat on top of my head. My face looked rounder, and you could just see the straps of my bikini. The shot on the poster ended at my shoulders, but it had been enlarged from a bigger picture, which I remembered Katie had taken of me out by the pool. My face was blurry.

The booking officer opened my wallet and pulled out the fake ID Cheryl had gotten me back when we were still friends. "Heaven Johnson?" she said, raising her eyes. I shrugged. "All right," she said. "Hank, call Detective Wachter. He's going to want to deal with this." She moved me down the counter and the lady cop undid my handcuffs.

They let me wash off my hands after the printing (that ink really stuck); then the lady cop led me down the hall to an interrogation room. I sat down at the metal table, cuffed again, and she left, banging the door closed behind her.

The room was cold. No windows, and a long mirror on one side that I knew must be one-way glass. I looked around for a camera. Yep. There was one up in the corner. One light hung down from the ceiling, casting a sickly glow.

After a few minutes the door opened and a tall, thin man wearing rumpled brown slacks and a white oxford shirt entered. His face was tired, and I guessed he must be about thirty-five—he looked like someone who didn't sleep very much.

"Hi, Heaven," he said. "I'm Detective Wachter. Karl Wachter." His eyes were very light blue. Fine lines showed around his mouth when he smiled. I decided his face looked kind.

"Hi," I said, shifting in my seat.

"I thought you might be hungry," he said, placing a bottle of water, a Coke, and a muffin on the table in front of me.

"Thanks," I said. He nodded, then came around behind me and unlocked my cuffs.

"Better?" he asked.

"Much," I said, rubbing my wrists. I stretched my arms above my head and opened the bottle of water, gulping it down, then sank my teeth into the muffin—blueberry. I chewed on it gratefully. I was starving, as usual. I tried not to fantasize about how good a plate of eggs and bacon would taste.

Detective Wachter sat down and arranged a tape recorder on the table in front of him. "So I'm sure you know we've been looking for you?"

"I saw my picture on the news a few months ago," I said through a mouthful of muffin. A few crumbs flew out of my mouth. "Sorry," I said, covering my mouth with my hand. "I'm really hungry."

"It's okay." He smiled. "Here's what we're going to do: You finish that up, and then I'm going to ask you to start at the beginning."

"What's the beginning?" I said, covering my mouth this time.

"Well, how about the night of the wedding?" Detective Wachter suggested, tapping his pen softly against the table. I was glad someone like him was interviewing me. It would make telling my story a whole lot easier. "One other thing," he said. "I'm going to have to tape this."

I choked a little on my muffin. "I don't understand—this isn't a confession." I swallowed. "Is it?"

"No. Although there is the matter of the stolen BMW."

"But we had no choice!" I said. "When those guys attacked us, we had to get out of there and—"

"Hold on, hold on," Detective Wachter soothed. "We'll get to that later. I'm taping you for your own protection, just to make sure we have a record of your story. And to make sure we have your story straight."

I wavered. Suddenly the reality of telling the authorities what I knew was overwhelming. It meant that I'd be telling them about the Kogos' dirty little yakuza secret. It meant that I'd no longer be in control of what happened next.

But wasn't that what I wanted?

"So the night of the wedding," Detective Wachter prompted, pressing the red "Record" button.

I stared at the tiny silver recorder. Yes. That was what I wanted.

"It kind of starts before that," I said, taking a swig of Coke. "And it's a really long story."

"I'm a good listener," he said. "Try me."

"Well," I began, "it started back in Tokyo when my father told me I was going to marry Teddy Yukemura. . . ."

It took longer than I thought to tell it. As the words poured out of me, I watched the detective's face, wondering if he believed them—they sounded strange even to me. I couldn't help imagining what I'd have been saying right now if things had been different, if my father *hadn't* arranged the marriage with Teddy—would Ohiko still be alive? I wondered if I'd have been living at the compound back in Tokyo, still basically clueless—useless. Or maybe the forces that had pursued me since then would have found their way into my life anyway. You can't escape your destiny, after all.

When I got to the part about Teddy's death, my voice stuck in my throat.

"They—they shot him . . . ," I stammered. "I just keep thinking about how the last time I said anything to him, I was angry—I was yelling at him to help me." I looked at Detective Wachter's understanding eyes. "I didn't know he'd been hurt." I gulped. "And now he's dead."

Detective Wachter looked puzzled for a second. "I'm sorry to make you go through all this," he said, "but can you tell me when was the last time you saw Teddy?"

"They threw him out the window," I said flatly. "Or maybe he jumped. He was bleeding."

"So it was in Tijuana?"

I nodded.

"Did you see the body?" Detective Wachter asked.

"No," I said. "It was gone when they led Hiro and me downstairs. Those people are animals." I took a sip of water. "Yoji didn't believe Teddy was dead."

"Wait—you talked to Yoji Yukemura?"

"Sorry. I'm getting ahead of myself." I continued my story, explaining how Hiro and I had escaped into San Diego and telling all about how Shigeto had led us to Yoji. I sketched out the conversation with Yoji, leaving out what had happened between him and Hiro before we left. I didn't want the police to get the wrong idea about Hiro.

Detective Wachter clicked the "Off" button on the tape recorder and cleared his throat. "Let's stop there for a second," he said. "There's something you need to know."

I stared at him. "Is it about my father?" I asked, my voice shaking. I'd had no news of him since leaving for Vegas—he might have finally awakened from his coma or he might be dead.

"No, it's not that," he said. "Teddy Yukemura is alive."

"What?" I gasped, stiffening in my chair. "That's impossible. I'm sure he went out the window!"

"Yes, I know. But you yourself said there was no body

143

when you and Hiro came downstairs. Our agents have seen Teddy here in L.A."

"No." I shook my head. "Teddy wouldn't have bailed on us like that. He cared too much about me."

"I'm sorry, Heaven, but it's true." He flipped open a folder and pushed it toward me. Inside was a stack of glossy black-and-white surveillance photos. Teddy walking into a nightclub. Teddy talking to a Hispanic man outside, their faces serious. Teddy and several other men getting into a car together. "These were taken last night at a club in North Hollywood—Autovox."

"I don't understand," I said, staring at the pictures as if the answers were hidden somewhere inside them. I was so happy that Teddy wasn't dead . . . but how could he have left me that way? "He was all bloody . . . ," I protested. "I *saw* it."

"He must have been pretending in order to escape. I don't know if you know about this, Heaven, but Teddy's wanted here on drug charges. We have evidence that he's been financing several big deals with Colombians from the Perezosa family."

So it was true. Teddy had lied to me. Something hot and bitter rose in the back of my throat, and I gripped the table hard to steady myself. He didn't really care about me—he was just a big, stinking drug dealer who was on the verge of getting his sorry ass busted. Maybe he'd hoped that once we all got to Paris, he'd be the new dealer in town. I felt sick to my stomach.

"I should have just come to you guys right after the wedding," I said, despair washing over me. "All I've done is to make a gigantic mess. No matter what I try to do, I always screw up—and all I've learned is that nobody tells the truth. Nobody." I looked up at Detective Wachter. "But you have to realize," I pleaded, wanting so much for one person, at least, to understand how all this had happened, "I was a different person then. I didn't know *anything*. All I knew was my father's house. I didn't even know he was yakuza!"

"We're going to try to help you, Heaven. But we'd like you to do something for us." He cleared his throat. "We need you to help us bring Teddy in."

"Like wear a wire or something?" I asked. The thought was appealing. Teddy was nothing more than a manipulative coward. I could see that now.

"Not exactly. We don't need any more evidence about the dealing. We just need to physically get our hands on him. Our agents lost track of him after he left Autovox last night. Teddy just—disappeared. We were hoping you'd be able to help us locate him."

"I have no idea where he is." *I wish I did so I could go find him and rip his head off,* I thought.

Detective Wachter frowned. "His cell phone number?"

I nodded. *"That,"* I said, "I do have. But what good will it do?"

"Well," Detective Wachter said, "that's where you come

in—you'll call him and set up a meeting, and then we'll arrest him."

So I was the bait. "And if I don't?" I said.

"Honestly?" Detective Wachter smiled a little sadly. "There's nothing we can do. The only thing we could charge you with is car theft, and even that wouldn't keep you here for long—and no one's registered the car as stolen yet. But you do need our protection. And frankly, I think you've underestimated how dangerous the Yukemuras are. What makes you so sure that they haven't orchestrated this whole thing? That Teddy wasn't just playing you back there in Vegas?"

I sighed. How *did* I know? All I had to go on was what I'd been told. But as pissed as I was at Teddy, I couldn't make myself believe he was totally evil and not just a goofball guy who secretly watched too many WB shows and felt like he could never live up to what his father wanted him to be. For goodness sake—he'd even *cried* when Ephram couldn't get anyone to believe that Colin was seriously messed up from his coma on *Everwood*. And in our hotel room at Joshua Tree he'd nearly peed in his pants when he saw the *America's Funniest Home Videos* clip of a tiny lizard in a party hat licking an ice-cream cone. Was that how a ruthless drug dealer behaved?

No. Teddy was spineless. A big, pathetic loser. And he deserved to get caught for saving his own ass and letting me think he'd been killed. But I knew he wasn't responsible for what had happened to Ohiko and my father. Thinking up a plan, much less a successful one, wasn't his thing.

"Does anything else happen to me if I don't want to do it?" Every last bit of me wanted to help—but I wanted to make sure I had all my options straight—it felt like the first time in ages I'd actually *had* options.

Detective Wachter looked serious. "I have superiors who are eager to get Teddy in custody—and we've been looking at him for a long time. If you decide not to help us, they could make things more difficult for you. Notify the INS—who might decide to involve the Japanese authorities." The detective raised his eyebrows. "And I think we both agree that *that* would be a bad thing."

"Definitely," I said, trying to process everything he was telling me. If the Japanese police became involved, the situation might blow up, and as soon as any of the yakuza families found out I was helping the police—it would be all over. There really *would* be a price on my head. Maybe more than one.

Time for me to cover my own butt for once.

"I'll do it," I said firmly.

"I'm glad to hear that," Detective Wachter said. He clicked the tape recorder back on. "How about telling me how you and Hiro ended up in the speeding BMW?"

I sketched out the rest of the story distractedly. Now that I knew Teddy was alive, everything was different. When Hiro and I got out of here, what would we do? Had Yoji really known that Teddy was alive all along? It certainly seemed that way, looking back on it. And if he'd lied about that . . . maybe he'd lied about everything.

"Great, Heaven," Detective Wachter said, looking at his watch. "I think it's time to wrap up."

"What time is it?" I asked.

"Noon," he said. I blinked in amazement. We'd been talking for almost four hours.

"Now what?" I asked.

"Well, the most important thing is to keep you safe—and this is the safest place there is. How do you feel about staying in a jail cell? It won't be the Beverly Wilshire, but I'll make sure you get a decent lunch and some extra blankets."

"As long as I don't have a roommate," I said. "But what about Hiro?"

"I'll find out," Detective Wachter said. He pressed a buzzer under the table, and the same woman cop came in and cuffed me again. "Sorry," she said apologetically. "Them's the rules."

We walked back through the lobby of the precinct, which had cleared out since earlier that morning. "Wow—it's so different," I said.

"Yeah, Sunday mornings are always the worst—we get a lot of business on Saturday nights," she said.

I hadn't even realized it was the weekend. When you had no job and nowhere to be, the days just kind of flowed together.

We walked into another wing of the station house, and she led me through a series of doors into what I realized was a cell block. I peeked into the cells as we walked by and saw groups of women sleeping on cots and benches behind the bars. Miss Thing was there, considerably less than seven feet tall now that she'd taken off her platforms. A lot of the girls were wearing short skirts or hot pants and push-up bras and were lolling on the wooden benches that lined the walls of the holding cell. With last night's makeup smudged and running, every single hooker looked like she had a pair of black eyes. And the banger chicks in their baggy jeans and bandannas seemed to actually have *been* beat up.

"Tell me I'm not going into a group cell," I said, edging away from the bars.

"Don't worry, honey," the cop said. "We're taking you to the maximum security unit."

"What?" I said, shocked. "Why?"

"Because it's empty," she said, looking amused. "You'll have your own room there. Nice and cozy."

"Hey, pretty girlie," yelled a girl about my age, huge boobs spilling out of her halter top. "Why don't you come in here with us?"

"Yeah, Officer," piped up another, "why's she so special?"

"Can it!" yelled the cop. "Behave yourselves."

Whistles and catcalls bounced off the walls around us

as we went through another door that was slammed and locked behind us. The guard slid open the bars and I stepped inside. The woman cop took off my handcuffs and then the bars slammed shut. It was just me, a toilet, a sink, and a cot. In a few minutes another guard came and opened a drawer in the bars, put a stack of blankets and a pillow inside it, then pushed it through to my side.

"This should make things a little easier," he said. I grabbed the pile of bedding, feeling like Hannibal Lecter or something. Couldn't I just have crashed on a couch in the break room or something? I shook out the first blanket and draped it over the cot. Then another. I threw the pillow on the bed and was just about to lie down when I heard the sound of bars sliding open somewhere down the hallway. A moment later Hiro walked by, led by another officer.

"Hiro!" I shouted, and ran over to the bars of the cell. I reached my arms through, but his hands were cuffed and he couldn't touch me. I gripped the bars instead, searching his face for clues about what he might have said to them.

"They're releasing me, Heaven," he said, his face pale. "You told them everything." It was a statement, not a question.

"Yes," I said. "It was the only thing to do."

"Are you okay?" he asked. It occurred to me that Hiro was the only person in the world right then who cared. I nodded. Part of me wanted to reach out and touch Hiro's sad face to comfort him, but something else held me back. I stepped away from the bars. Couldn't he see that there was no other option? Why was that so hard for him to understand? After all, he could walk right on out of the police station and never look back if he wanted to—wash his hands of me once and for all.

"Heaven—are you sure it was the right thing to do?"

"Teddy's alive," I said flatly.

Hiro's eyes widened. "Are you sure? How do you—"

"I just know," I said sharply, cutting him off. "Take my word for it."

Hiro shook his head. "It doesn't change anything. Who cares what he does?"

I'd never heard Hiro talk like that about another person. I'd just told him that Teddy was alive, but I might as well have told him my nose itched for all it affected him.

"The main thing is, we don't know what the police will do with the information, Heaven," he continued. "Heaven?" he asked as I moved farther away from the bars. When I looked into his eyes, I couldn't stop thinking about how he'd lied to me about his family's yakuza history, and it seemed to me he'd done it because he just loved playing the good guy too much. Hadn't I thought he was selfish when I'd first begun training with him? Maybe I'd been right. At least Teddy hadn't pretended to be what he wasn't.

"It's over, Hiro," I said, tiredness washing over me. I realized that when I looked at him, I felt—nothing. Just empty. "I can't do this anymore," I said, not exactly sure what that meant, only knowing that it was true.

Hiro's eyes glistened, but he stepped back and allowed the guard to lead him down the hallway.

I hurled myself onto the bed and sobbed.

They're taking me to a motel. The last place I want to be right now. I asked them why I couldn't just go home—now that the place has been ransacked, I don't think they'll be coming back for more. Besides, I'm sure the guys in the SUV that was trailing us spread the word that we were taken into police custody. But no, they said, it wouldn't be safe. As if it were *my* safety I cared about.

It's Heaven they need to worry about. I could see the pain in her eyes. It was a mistake not to tell her my story—a big mistake. But when was there time? First there was Karen, and Heaven's training, and then the madness that started in Joshua Tree that hasn't let up since. We always had so many other things to discuss—there wasn't time to talk about the past.

When they've given me my room key and stationed the guard outside, I step into the shower and wash the pain of our last battle off me. It's deep. Watching the droplets of water bounce off the tiles, a moment of clarity opens up before me—there *was* time. There was plenty of time to tell her. I could have said something when we were driving back from San Diego. I could have whispered it to her over our meal at the diner before Cheryl showed up—even in the hotel room back in Mexico. The truth was that by then, I didn't want her to know. I allowed my pride to take over—the way she looked at me was intoxicating. I'd never felt that bond with anyone, knowing how much she loved me and how much I loved her back—it was like a drug.

The truth is, I was afraid. Afraid she would hate me if I told her. Think less of me.

And she does. But not because my father is yakuza.

No. It's because I lied to her, just like everybody else did.

I lean my head against the wall. How could I have been so stupid?

All I want to do now is sleep, to escape. The motel room is gray and shabby; I can feel the residue of the lives that have passed through this room, which is a prison in its own right. Across town Heaven's sitting on that cot in that cold cell, all alone.

I left Japan so that I'd never have to feel this kind of despair again. And even though it was lonely and difficult when I arrived in California, there was always hope. I can't seem to muster any of that just now. I keep thinking back to Kyoto, and how I was so lost then. But at least I knew I was looking for answers. In the Shinto religion, fire is sacred. It has the power to destroy evil, and this sacred power is celebrated yearly in the hi matsuri, or fire festival. Fire also signals the ascent of the deity, the god or goddess. Flame destroys so that new life can be born. The dual nature of the flame instructs us on the dual nature of our own paths. Back then, I still believed there was one path for me. But now I think I might have lost my way.

I draw the curtains closed, blocking out the early afternoon light. If only I could go to her, fly across town and into her cell, tell her how sorry I am. How weak it was of me to deny where and what I came from and to hide a part of my soul from her. But I can't. I'm stuck. I have to stay here and sleep. Clear my thoughts, find the path that will lead me out of this maze.

Tomorrow, tomorrow . . .

Hiro

12

The smell of damp brick. Scratchy wool under my cheek. Voices murmuring in fear. I reached out to touch Hiro's warm, sleeping body.

My eyes snapped open. No Hiro. No nothing. Gunmetal gray ceiling. Where was I?

"Heaven?" A warm voice called to me in Japanese. I must have been dreaming. "Nagai aida o-me ni kakari-masen deshita. It's been a long time."

I sat up quickly, the heavy, rough blankets puddling around my waist. My hair and T-shirt were damp with sweat. Jail. I was in an L.A. jail. A thin, weathered-looking Japanese man stood at the bars of the cell. He was dressed in an expensive suit and wore small wire-framed glasses. He looked vaguely familiar. . . . I closed my eyes. Was he some sort of spirit sent to comfort me in my sleep?

But when I opened them again, he was still there. Suddenly it all came rushing back to me. Masato. Mieko's brother. My uncle. I'd met him for the first time the night of the wedding—well, not met, really. But I remembered staring at him curiously as my father walked me up the aisle. Growing up, I'd always heard about Uncle Masato, knew that he ran the Kogo interests in Central America. But he'd never come to Japan to visit for as long as I'd been around.

"Masato-san," I said, bowing, my voice cracking a little. It was partly my sleepiness, partly emotion—it was unexpectedly comforting to see someone from my family after all this time, even a family member who was a stranger to me—and Mieko's brother, no less.

"The police called your stepmother to notify her that you had been found," Masato said. He spoke formally and stood so straight that he looked like he was about to deliver a speech to a board of directors, not hunker down for a chat in a prison cell. "She asked me to come see you." Footsteps echoed in the hallway and soon a guard appeared to unlock the door. We were led to an interview room (a different one, this time), and I sat down across from my uncle.

"I've spoken with Detective Wachter. I've assured him that every measure will be taken to ensure your safety if you decide to place yourself under my protection."

"Thank you, Uncle," I said, bowing again. I was trying to make a good impression, but I wasn't quite sure what

Masato was suggesting. "Did the detective tell you about Teddy Yukemura?"

"Ah, yes . . . young Takeda. It's really a shame about that boy. He's made quite a mess of his life. The detective told me you wish to help the police get their hands on him?"

I nodded.

Masato sighed. "I can't say I approve of them having you do their dirty work for them, but on the other hand, they could make it much smoother for you to get out of the country in—I believe they say, 'one piece'?"

"So you think it's the right thing to do?" I asked, studying my uncle's face. I could definitely see his resemblance to Mieko—similar eyes and that surprisingly delicate nose . . . and he had a dose of her coldness and reserve. But there was a spark to Masato that I'd never seen in Mieko—some deeper fire that burned inside him that powered him. Both were outwardly still people, but where Mieko was languid, Masato looked wound up tight.

"Right, wrong—who can say? But the Yukemura boy has it coming to him anyway . . . and by leaving you, shall we say, 'in the lurch,' he's proved himself nothing more than a selfish coward. Perhaps finally being caught will even help him—Yoji Yukemura and his silly wife always did spoil that boy. From what your stepmother has told me, they absolutely *ruined* him with their attentions."

I listened, fascinated. None of the adults in my family, or in my family's circle, had *ever* spoken to me of things like that. I sensed that my uncle Masato was the kind of person who liked to gossip—so at least we had one thing in common. But why was Masato still in the U.S.?

"And after *that* unpleasant business," Masato continued, "I'll take you back to Japan. You can stay in my villa until we get this situation under control. You'll be perfectly safe."

"Forgive me Masato-san," I said, "I know you attended my wedding, but have you remained in the U.S. all this time?"

"No, no, of course not." Masato spread his hands flat on the table and inspected his nails thoughtfully. "I flew back to Costa Rica immediately after the ceremony. I was of no use to anyone here. But as soon as I heard that your father had been attacked and was in a coma, I boarded a plane to Japan to help my sister—your stepmother, of course—proceed with the appropriate administration of the Kogo interests."

It was news to me that Mieko had been handling my father's business. I'd never imagined my frivolous, subservient stepmother being capable of that—she could administer her shoe rack, and that was about it. I assumed that Masato must be pretty much handling everything, but that was a little odd, too—after all, my father had several close advisers who had to be more familiar with the day-to-day operations of Kogo Industries in Japan than Masato could be after twenty years out of the country.

THE BOOK OF THE FLAME

159

"How is my father?" I asked quietly.

"Konishi is much the same. Some of the doctors think he will wake up any day, others say the prospects are grim. You know these physicians, with their fancy degrees"—Masato waved one manicured hand dismissively—"nobody knows anything. They poke and prod with their instruments, but at the end of the day their guess is only as good as anybody else's." Masato sighed. He was quite a character. And I sensed that he was in no hurry to have my father wake up. The question was, how was Masato going to protect me from Mieko? I wanted to ask him, but I decided to wait until I had a better idea of exactly how close he and Mieko were at this point.

"Do you know who sent the ninja to the wedding?" I asked.

"Mieko and I have put the best men on it. Or rather, I *myself* have been leading an investigation that I believe is almost complete. You know your stepmother can be, shall we say, something of a hindrance in these matters."

I smiled. Did I ever. Mieko was a chronic naysayer—no matter what was suggested, she always acted like you'd asked her to do something totally inconceivable—like wear black with navy blue or something tragic like that.

"I'm almost positive we've discovered the culprit, Heaven," Masato said, pushing his small glasses up on his nose. "A traitor—someone who is very close to the Kogo family. Someone with enough knowledge to make it look as if Konishi himself was responsible."

"Who?" I asked, flipping through a mental Rolodex of my father's closest advisers and friends.

"Ah, ah, ah," Masato said, wagging his finger at me. "All in good time. When we return to Japan, I will let you read the evidence we have amassed. Then you will see the face of the man who planned these attacks . . . and you can have your revenge."

"How long do you think it will be before you can act?" I asked, clenching my fists. Just *thinking* about the people who had killed my brother made my arms and legs tingle the way they always did just before a fight.

"A month, maybe less." Masato shrugged, then leaned forward. "That is why you must come with me back to Japan. You'll be much safer there than here in the U.S. Plus you'll be there when your father wakes up. Right at his bed-side."

"*If* he wakes up," I said dully. With each day that passed, I was losing hope that he ever would.

"He's going to wake up—you have to believe it. Your father is a strong man. Imagine that he's simply conserving his impressive strength right now, coiling it around him like the cobra before it strikes!" Masato raised his fist, eyes blazing, and I shrank back in my chair a little bit. There was definitely a fury inside him—and that might make him the perfect ally. On the other hand . . . I had no idea how deep Masato's own yakuza connection went. He could be as twisted as the rest of them—and there was no guarantee that if my father didn't wake up, Masato would end the Kogo-Yukemura feud.

"With all due respect, Uncle," I said tentatively, rubbing my tired eyes, "in the last few months I've learned all about Kogo Industries—*all* about it. Maybe I was naive, but learning about what our family does has been a shock to me." I knew I was walking a fine line—I wanted him to feel he could tell me the truth about our family, let me know if he, too, disapproved, but I didn't want to scare him away from letting me know how things *really* stood.

Masato studied me for a moment, his eyes hard and steely behind the shiny lenses of his glasses. "Do you know why I became head of the Kogo operations in Central America?" he asked.

I shook my head. "I have no idea. No one ever spoke of it."

"No, they wouldn't have," Masato said thoughtfully, staring off into the distance. "The truth is that I learned what your father was up to only after I started working for him. By that time he was engaged to my sister—the match had been announced, the ceremonial clothing was being made. . . . I begged her not to marry him when I found out about his . . ."

"Yakuza connection?" I offered.

"Tsk, tsk," Masato clicked, "such a nasty word. Shall we say, his particular 'brand of business'? Things were much different back then. None of this running around that young people do today. Back in our day, once the engagement was announced, that was the end of it. To break the engagement would have brought great shame to our family. Mieko would never have found another suitable match. She would have appeared to be 'damaged goods,' as they say."

In spite of myself, I made a face. Maybe that explained why Mieko had been so unsympathetic when Konishi had announced that I would marry Teddy. She probably figured if she'd had to do her duty, then I could do it, too.

"Distasteful, I know, but sadly, the truth," Masato continued. "I vowed to continue working for 'the business' in hopes that I could ultimately convince Konishi to follow the, as they say, 'straight and narrow.' I thought that once Mieko knew she was going to have a child—your poor brother, Ohiko—that Konishi would change his ways. But he was in too deep. He brushed me off like a fly whenever I spoke to him about it. Yes, just like a fly, swatting me away with no more thought than if I had been a tiny, buzzing insect."

I stared at Masato. There was no malice in his voice. It was as if he was telling a story that had happened to someone else, that he had heard once long, long, ago, and one that now made no difference to him whatsoever. His lack of bitterness surprised me—I knew how it felt to fight against something and feel like no one was listening. I spent a lot of time feeling like that.

"But you know," Masato continued, "Kogo Industries owns a great number of legitimate business operations.

The farther one gets from Japan, the looser the hold of those disturbing elements you mentioned earlier. In fact, that is how I ended up in Central America—your father was tired of hearing my complaints. He didn't want to be reminded that once he was the type of man who would have scorned any association with such bottom-feeders. So he shipped me off to handle the Central American operations, and after a time I learned to love Costa Rica, Guatemala, Nicaragua. I was traveling constantly, and before I knew it, the years had passed and I'd built a life for myself."

"Didn't you miss Japan?" I asked, trying to imagine how I would feel if I knew I had to stay in the States for the rest of my life.

"At first," Masato answered slowly, "of course. I found the Central Americans barbaric and their food appalling. But regardless of all else, your father is a generous man. I was being paid handsomely. I had a house built in the Japanese style, and a chef was sent over from Tokyo to prepare my meals. Handled correctly, the seafood in Costa Rica is stupendous. I learned to appreciate the beauty of my surroundings—so wild and carefree. I knew if I returned, it would only cause problems for your mother, so I stayed away. Our parents were dead, I had no wife. . . . On vacations I would go to New York City, or Tuscany, or skiing in Switzerland. Yes, a very nice life, all things considered. I have no regrets."

I rubbed my eyes again, trying to keep my thinking

straight. "Do you think my father could be convinced to break with the yak—the 'bad elements'?" I asked, remembering at the last minute my uncle's distaste for the word.

"Why not? I'm sure his brush with death will cause him to rearrange his priorities. It is always so. And from what I understand, he dotes on you."

"I don't know about that," I said, forgetting for a second that I was trying to be polite. Doting was not really up Konishi Kogo's alley.

Masato ignored me. "Perhaps if you come back to Japan and are with him during his recovery, he will agree to, shall we say, 'go straight.' Especially after all that's happened—it might just be enough to make him see reason after all these years."

"Do you really think so?" I asked, cringing at the childish, hopeful sound of my own voice. I wanted nothing more than to have my father back, and to have him back the way he was before I knew about his real business. Back when he was just a very wealthy businessman and a strict, sometimes even harsh, father. That was better than having him be a crime lord.

"Who knows?" Masato said, gently shrugging again, in what I was realizing was a trademark gesture of his, almost a tic. "He is growing old now, and with Ohiko gone, he has far less to lose by cutting ties. They've already struck at the roots of his tree—why not shake off a few more leaves?"

"Why not?" I echoed Masato's words. I wanted to believe that such a future was possible.

"So . . . ," Masato said, his silky-smooth voice lulling me deeper into my fatigue, "will you accompany me back to Japan?"

I stared down at the table. I was feeling groggy and confused, and Masato's words seemed to float in my head in a big, disconnected mass. I couldn't really make sense of what he had told me, although I understood it. It was like my brain had stopped being able to process how his story fit in with everything else I knew. I tried to concentrate—now it seemed clear that the Yukemuras had been responsible for everything. But back in Yoji's hotel suite, I'd been equally convinced that there were other, unknown forces eager to destroy the Kogos *and* the Yukemuras.

Then again, I'd been wrong a lot more than I'd been right over the past few days. Maybe it was time to accept that whoever it was I was running from, my family was the safest place to run to.

And then there was Masato, my newfound uncle—what to make of him? I peeked across the table. He was thin and somewhat frail looking, and as I watched, he picked a piece of lint calmly off his pants and flicked it toward the corner, his nostrils flaring slightly. I got the impression he was finicky—certainly not imposing in the way my father was—a bit weak, perhaps. He didn't seem particularly kind, but he wasn't cruel. Maybe a little sad and lonely, affected, kind of professorial . . .

Aaaaagh—my mind was wandering. I stopped looking at him and focused again on the table, trying to let the web of perception I'd gained access to do the work for me. But I was drawing a blank. My nerves were frayed. The reception was foggy. I was operating on not nearly enough sleep. Come to think of it, how long *had* I slept? Five hours? Less?

"What time is it?" I asked, realizing all at once that I was dangling out of time again and wondering suddenly about Hiro.

Masato looked at his watch. "Eight o'clock. Time for dinner. If you leave with me now, I'll have something delicious brought to your hotel room. The finest sushi and an excellent sake. We'll celebrate the end of this little adventure of yours. And you can take care of police business tomorrow."

"And when we get back to Japan?" I asked. "Will I be free to do whatever I choose?"

Masato raised his eyebrows. "What do you mean?"

I plucked up my courage. "Will I be able to go to university? Keep my own schedule? See who I please?"

"Ah." Masato adjusted his suit coat. "I think I can assure you that your stepmother wants nothing so much as your happiness. I see no reason why you should not be able to continue your education. As for the other freedoms . . . certainly you can go shopping, visit restaurants. With bodyguards, of course. At least until we have this, ahem, unfortunate situation under control."

For the first time I thought about what it would actually mean for me to be going back to Japan—it meant going back to all the luxuries I'd done without all this time. A chef, good food on demand. A change of clothes every day and more than that if I wanted it. What's more, I could live the life I'd always wished Konishi would let me have. I could apply to university and get my degree—art history, maybe. And in the meantime there'd be leisure. Swimming and reading magazines and . . . and . . .

Not much else. Ohiko was gone. Katie was in Vegas. I had no friends. Mieko didn't like me, even if she wasn't trying to kill me. And Hiro.

"What about—" I started, then caught myself.

"Yes?" Masato said, raising his eyebrows expectantly.

I'd been about to ask where Hiro was. But suddenly I didn't want to know. Time enough to ask about that tomorrow. I felt like I had to make this decision on my own. Whatever happened between Hiro and me, it would have to fit into the choices I was making for myself. For my *own* life.

"With all respect, Uncle, I need some time to think about this decision," I said, speaking as formally as I could—the way I used to talk to my father. "I appreciate your offer, and I know you want the best for me. Could you possibly come back tomorrow? I'll give you my decision then."

"Do you really want to spend any more time in this

wretched place?" Masato asked, his face faintly disgusted. "Why not come with me and think about it later?"

"I need to be alone now to sleep and meditate," I said.

"Very well," Masato said, pushing his chair back from the table. I could tell all the talk about dinner had made him eager to get on with his own. "You decide whether you want to accompany me back to Japan. If you do, I will return the day after tomorrow on my way to the airport. A ticket will be ready for you should you decide to use it. If you prefer to come with me earlier and leave the police to their own little shenanigans with Takeda, just tell that detective—I'll send a chauffeur to pick you up whenever you call, day or night." He stood up. "Which I highly recommend you do."

I stood. "Domo arigato—thank you, Uncle," I said, bowing. "I enjoyed our talk, and I appreciate you being so honest with me."

"I trust I will see you soon, niece." Masato rapped on the door and the guard came in. With another bow Masato was gone, and I was taken back down the long hallway to my cell.

Dude, I could not believe it when Heaven called me! That's insane! I mean, I was sure I'd really screwed the pooch on that last one. Yeah, it sucked that I left her in Tijuana or whatever, but I figured they wouldn't hurt her. They wanted her alive—I knew that, or else I would have gone down fighting. I mean, when all's said and done, I still love the lady, you know?

But man, I was just so pissed about that stupid Hiro thing! What is she thinking? The guy's a loser with a capital L-O-S-E-R. He's all, like, Mr. Silent Tough Guy Jet Li. Whatever. Kiss my badass butt, G. I mean, come on. That shit's so old school, it's not even cool. And she totally bought it just because the cat looks good in a pair of motorcycle pants. Big friggin' deal. Where I come from, he'd get his ass housed in about ten seconds.

She said one of my peeps called her with my number. I wonder who it was? I mean, I know I talk about her a lot, but still. Seems weird that Max or Rico would do something like that. Anyway, sounds like this Hiro's out of the picture now, and she's ready for some Teddy-style lovin'. I told her we could still leave the country like we planned and get married. I just need to finish this one last deal, and then we'll have such mad bank we won't need jack from no-body. We'll set up house in Switzerland or something and I'll treat her like a queen. Just me 'n' her. It'll be awesome.

I think she was pretty into it. She was so cute, all, like, 'Teddy, you scared me to death! I thought you were dead!' It was nice to know she cared 'cause honestly, when I crawled my sorry butt off that dusty patch of Mexico, I thought she'd never want to see me again.

I did kind of leave them in a spot there. . . .

But whatever. No harm done. Teddy Yo Yo YO is back in action! We're going to meet up tomorrow out at the planetarium—I'll give her a wad of cash so she can get pretty and a ticket—and the passport. I took those with me when I ran. We'll meet up in Paris, first, I think, and get married there.

It'll be like a music video. We'll get married on the Eiffel Tower or in Notre Dame or somethin'. Real blingy, with fine wine and lots of partyin'. I'll be so loaded, I won't be able to see straight. With cash, I mean, not the liquor. I don't think she's a big boozer, but that's okay. She's not some useless party ho—I'm done with those.

She's mine. My piece of Heaven. And I'll get to see her tomorrow night.

Can't wait.

13

The control room was packed. Plainclothes detectives and cops in uniform ran back and forth among the tightly crammed desks, and up on the wall hung a huge map of the planetarium grounds stuck with pushpins. (I only knew it was the planetarium because someone had written PLANE-TARIUM at the top in big, sprawling, Magic Marker letters.) After an afternoon and night of tossing, turning, and thinking on my cot, the activity was something of a shock. I was grateful when Detective Wachter loomed up out of the chaos.

"Heaven, come this way," he said gently, taking my arm and leading me through the crowd. As we walked through the room, the people we passed stopped talking and stared.

"Why are they staring at us?" I whispered.

"They all know who you are," Detective Wachter said. "You're something of a legend around here, you know. We've been looking for you for months."

It was a strange feeling—almost nostalgic. Back in Japan, I'd been something of a celebrity. Not only had I been the sole survivor of that plane crash, but I was Konishi Kogo's daughter—and my father was a household name. In Tokyo, at least. But I'd had no idea that so much effort had been put into finding me here in the U.S. If I *had* known, I would have given up a long time ago.

And now all these people were searching for Teddy. And I was going to help them.

"This is Detective Martin—she's going to be explaining all the details of the sting to you." Detective Wachter led me to a desk behind which sat a woman with short, dark brown hair and wide eyes. She stood up and held out her hand, and when I took it, she gripped my hand in a power grip. Detective Martin was hot—about three inches taller than me—and I instinctively looked from her to Detective Wachter and back again. Was something going on there?

"Hi, Heaven. We really appreciate you helping us out with this."

"No problem," I said, with slightly more confidence than I felt. I didn't feel like I'd done a very good job with the Teddy phone call—at first I'd been so angry, I could barely control my shaking voice. But he'd agreed to meet me immediately. Maybe when I finally saw him, I'd clue him in that drug dealers should really be a bit more selective about these things. Moron.

"Well, we do appreciate it," Detective Wachter said. "Should we get started?"

"Right," Detective Martin said, gesturing to a chair by her desk. We sat down, and Detective Wachter perched on the edge of a nearby desk. "As you already know, we're going to carry out the sting at the planetarium." I nodded. We were supposed to meet there that night.

"How are you guys going to deal with the crowd?" I asked. "I mean, won't it be kind of weird to bust in if there are people around?"

Detective Martin smiled. "The planetarium is closed right now for renovations. There may be a few visitors looking at the view, but we'll send in a team to make sure it's cleared out beforehand. We're going to block the road that leads up to the site, so the only people who'll get through will be us and Teddy."

"And a lot of cops," I added. "Right?"

"Right," Detective Wachter said. "So you'll have nothing to worry about. We'll be watching you every step of the way."

"So the question is—do you want to wear a wire? Like Detective Wachter told you, we don't need the evidence— we've got plenty of that. But if you're wired, we'll know immediately if something starts to go wrong."

"Like what?" I said.

"Well, if Teddy tries to get rough with you, for instance."

"I don't think *that* will happen," I said wryly. "He likes me *in that way*, if you know what I mean."

"Still . . . ," Detective Wachter said, "it's something you should think about."

"No," I said firmly, "I'll be fine." There were a few things I wanted to ask Teddy about. And I certainly didn't want the police listening in on stuff that had absolutely nothing to do with them.

"But you have to remember," Detective Martin said, her face serious, "if you're not going to be wired, we won't be able to track your conversation. That means that if you're scared for your safety, we need to have an agreed-upon sign so that we'll know to come in and stop the sting."

I had to resist a smile at that one—I certainly couldn't imagine that a chat with Teddy would end with me fearing for my life. Not unless he tried to kiss me or something.

"Something funny?" Detective Wachter asked.

"No, sorry," I said, biting my lip. "So what's the sign?"

"It can be anything you're comfortable with, really," Detective Martin said. "But it has to be a broad movement that can be seen by our lookouts—and one that won't be misunderstood."

"How about a hat?" I suggested.

"A hat?" Detective Martin said, looking confused for a second.

"Yeah, like a baseball cap," I said, warming up to the

idea. "I'll wear it to the meeting, and if things get too wiggy, I'll take it off. It'll be obvious I'm in trouble."

The detectives looked at each other. "She's good," Detective Wachter said with a grin.

"Agreed," Detective Martin said. I felt stupidly proud. Maybe in another life I could have been a detective myself. Detective Kogo, keeping the peace in the City of Angels.

But no. In this life I was just a stool pigeon.

"All right," Detective Martin said, standing up. "I'll tell the team what we've decided about the signal. Other than that, you need to keep Teddy there for about seven and a half minutes—that's how long we need before we'll be able to get the teams in sync and go in. Here's a watch. Make sure you check your time—it can drag."

"Okay." I strapped the watch onto my wrist. "No problem."

"So that's really it," Detective Wachter said. "We'll be ready to go in an hour or so." He looked down at me. "Do you want to hang out here until then?"

"If you don't mind," I said. I didn't feel like being alone anymore. I was ready to do what I needed to do, and I wanted to stay pumped.

Detective Martin smiled. "I don't blame you. Do you want a magazine or something?" She opened the drawer of her desk and pulled out a stack of *People* magazines.

"Oh, awesome," I breathed. "It's been a long time since I've had my fill of celebrity gossip."

"Enjoy," Detective Wachter said as he walked away. But I was already lost in the sordid tale of Ben and J.Lo's latest breakup . . . other people's lives were always so much easier to think about.

"Are you sure you're okay with this, Heaven?"

"Fine," I said shortly, propping my foot against the backseat and tying my shoelace. Now I just wanted the whole thing to be over. Back at the precinct, it had all seemed like some bizarre game. Now the reality of what I was about to do was sinking in. I dropped my foot and toyed nervously with the bill of the baseball cap they'd given me. *Teddy deserves it,* I told myself, and tried to access the anger I'd felt when I'd realized how he'd abandoned me. But I was having trouble getting there.

"Now, listen, if anything seems strange to you— *anything*—I want you to get out of there as fast as you can. Like I said, we need seven and a half minutes to get prepared— but you have to trust your instincts. If something seems off, we'll send an officer in solo." Detective Wachter seemed way more nervous than I was. I had the feeling he had a lot riding on being able to nab Teddy, maybe a promotion or something. He piloted the car toward the planetarium. Fifteen minutes to go before my scheduled eight o'clock rendezvous with Teddy.

From the conversations we'd had on the way over, I'd gotten the impression that the detective thought Teddy was a lot more dangerous than he was. He didn't realize that the only scary thing about Teddy was that if you put a gun in his hand, he might fire it the wrong way and blow his own foot off—or your foot. The Mexico thing was typical Teddy—I should have known he'd chicken out when it came down to it. It was just like at the wedding. When the ninja had dropped in through the skylight, Teddy had first hidden behind me, then bolted, leaving me stranded right in the ninja's path before Ohiko had burst out of the wings and taken him on.

We pulled into the parking lot. A sign said Griffith Planetarium and Observatory: Closed Until 2005.

"Are you positive you don't want to wear a wire, Heaven?" Detective Martin turned around in her seat, frowning. "There's still time to get one of the guys to set you up with one."

"No, thanks," I said, looking out my window at the large domes of the building. It was exciting to finally see it. *Rebel Without a Cause* was one of my favorite movies, and I'd always dreamed of coming to see the planetarium where they'd filmed some of the best scenes—the class field trip, where James Dean meets Natalie Wood . . . and the final, tragic denouement. . . . It was so romantic. I almost wished it *wasn't* closed so I could go watch the planet show inside. I'd always wanted to see one of those.

"We'll wait here until we get the word that everyone's in place," Detective Wachter said, pulling a can of Coke from a bag at his side.

The plan was so simple. I was the bait, Teddy was the

fish. I could walk in, walk out, and tomorrow I'd be on a flight to Japan, leaving this life behind.

"It's time," Detective Martin said, ruffling her fingers in her short dark hair. "You set?"

"Ten-four," I said, trying to smile.

"All right, kiddo, go for it," Detective Wachter said, chucking his empty Coke can out the window into a trash can. "We're right here. Remember that."

I stepped out of the unmarked police car and slammed the door behind me. I adjusted the white L.A. Dodgers cap on my head and regretted for a moment that I'd suggested the hat thing. It felt a little silly, but it really was the easiest thing for me to remember. Not that I thought I'd need to give "the sign." The idea was absurd.

It was dark, and the place was deserted. The police had seen to that earlier. I felt a little exposed as I climbed the steps to the outlook by myself. The lights of the city were on, and I wandered toward the edge of the little plaza to take it all in. Teddy would be here any minute, and I wanted to think.

Was I betraying Teddy? That was really the question. Of course I was. But he had betrayed me. One way or another, everyone had betrayed me. Cheryl, Teddy . . . even Hiro. Detective Wachter had told me that he was still staying in the motel—but that he wanted to see me. Whether or not I wanted to see him was a question I was still not able to answer.

"Heaven, whassup?" Teddy wrapped his arms around my waist. I was enveloped in the smell of hair gel and new leather.

I stepped away. "Hi, Teddy," I said, trying to control my shaking voice. "Where have you been?" I gritted my teeth, swallowing the stream of insults I wanted to shout at him. *You stupid loser! You idiot! How could you let me think you'd been killed? Do you even know what that feels like?*

No. I was supposed to make chitchat—that was my job. And I wasn't going to find out just what *had* happened to Teddy down in Mexico if I started cursing him out. I glanced down at my watch—8:01. I had to make it to 8:09, more or less.

"Oh, man, Heaven. It was so *crazy*." Teddy plopped himself down on the low wall and motioned for me to take a seat next to him, which I did. "Hey! Your hair!" Teddy reached over and grabbed the bill of my hat.

"No!" I yelped as he tried to take it off. I took out some of my aggression by slapping his hand away as hard as I could.

"Ow!" Teddy rubbed his hand. "You don't want to show me?" He looked hurt.

"Um . . . no, it's just—bad hair day. I'm still getting used to it. I'll show you later, okay?"

"All right," Teddy said, grinning. "I know how that goes. I'll have plenty of time to get used to it later."

"Uh-huh," I said, my heart pounding in my chest. What

a disaster *that* would have been if he'd managed to tip my cap off.

"It's pretty short, though, huh?" Teddy said, trying to peek around the cap.

"Yeah, no kidding," I said sarcastically. But my anger was dissolving. Teddy was just so . . . *Teddy*. Whatever his flaws, it was nice that you always knew what to expect with him. "I had to go undercover. You don't like it?" I asked, striking a pose. "I mean, don't you think the hat thing is kind of fly?"

"No, man, that's not what I meant. It's cool, it's cool. It's kind of like, hot anime chick, you know? You're like, Princess Mononoke. I mean, that's what I *think* it would look like—I mean, if I could see it, I bet it would be like that. Or something."

"Thanks, Teddy." I cut him off before he could come up with more cartoon characters to compare me to. "Now where the hell have you been?"

"Oh, Heaven," Teddy pleaded, rubbing my back, "I'm so sorry I left you in Mexico—but I knew they wouldn't hurt you. Me, on the other hand—those guys wanted me *D-E-A-D*."

"Why?" I asked, moving out of his range. "I mean, where did everything go wrong? One minute you were off picking up the passports and the next you were bursting into the hotel room with those thugs. Were they drug dealers or what?" I checked my watch—only a few more minutes to go. I needed to find out what had *really* happened down in Tijuana—and fast.

"They weren't drug dealers, Heaven." Teddy shook his head. "That's a whole different bag of tricks. I've got those guys under my *thumb*. The guys with me that day were Yukemura men."

"What?" I gasped. "Teddy, how could you do such a thing? You traitor!" I yelled, standing up before I remembered that might freak out the cops. I sat down again.

"But—but don't you see?" Teddy stammered. "I had to! I knew they wouldn't hurt you or I wouldn't have showed them where you and Hiro were staying. My pops told me if I didn't deliver you, he'd have us all killed."

"Your father said that?" I asked, unbelieving.

"Yep. So I figured, 'Hey, I know he's not going to kill my Heaven, so I'll just let this go down, get the passports, and catch up with my baby later.' And see," Teddy continued, draping an arm around my shoulders, "it all worked out for the best."

"Your father lied to me. He told me he didn't know who was after me." I pushed Teddy's arm off me. He had a lot of nerve being all lovey-dovey with me while basically admitting that he'd screwed me over big time. And Yoji—he hadn't become oyabun of the Yukemuras for nothing. So slippery—he'd fooled Hiro and me completely.

Teddy shrugged. "He lies all the time. What else is new?"

I stared at Teddy and it struck me all over again. We were both being used. No matter what we did, they always found a way to trap us.

"Here's what, though," Teddy continued. "Me and you are *finished* with this bullshit, baby. I've got your ticket to Pa-ree right here, a passport, and some cash. You can go shopping. I'll be there in a few days—name of the hotel's in here." He fished in his oversized leather coat emblazoned with the number 310—the Beverly Hills area code, cheesily enough—and pulled out a thick brown envelope.

I stared at it.

"Go on, girl, take it," Teddy cajoled, rubbing my shoulder. "Don't be shy. Here." He pushed the envelope into my hands.

But I couldn't do it. I wasn't like him. Wasn't like the rest of them, taking the money, taking the deal, sucking it up. In all of this . . . this *wretchedness*, I'd almost managed to forget that I was a warrior, a samurai. I had something that none of these people had—honor. And if I gave that up, then I might as well die myself. Because I'd be just as bad as they were.

"No, no!" I said, suddenly springing to life and pushing the envelope back at him. "Listen to me, Teddy." I grabbed the collar of his jacket and pulled him toward me, knowing that at any minute Detective Wachter and his crew would be swarming all over the place. "It's a setup. They're using me to get to you. The police caught me—two days ago. I told them everything—I thought you were dead. And now they're trying to arrest you for a drug deal."

"What?" Teddy scanned the pavilion. "I don't see anyone. I don't get it."

"Please, Teddy," I begged, pushing the envelope back toward him. "You have to get out of here. In a minute they'll be everywhere."

"Are you playin'?" Teddy asked.

Come on, Teddy, I thought. *Get a grip. Don't be such a moron for once in your life.*

"I am *so* not playing, Teddy," I said, tears coming to my eyes when I thought about what I'd been about to do. "Get out of here. I'm sorry—go, go!" I hissed.

Teddy stood up, looking like he was in shock. "But what about Paris? When will I see you again?"

I shook my head. "Get out of here!"

Teddy stumbled toward me and grabbed my hand. "I'm sorry about Mexico, Heaven," he said.

"I know," I answered, looking desperately around me. "I *know. Leave!*" Teddy grabbed my head and kissed me on the cheek, knocking my cap off before he bolted across the pavilion. I scrabbled around on the ground and crushed the cap back on my head, praying that he'd make it back to his car before the police team came in.

And then suddenly—a figure in black, flying down as if from the sky.

Teddy was knocked to the ground.

"Go, go!" I heard the sound of doors slamming and foot-steps and stood, mesmerized, as the figure in black approached me.

Ninja.

Not again, I thought. *Not now.*

But it was now. It was right now. The black-clad figure bounded toward me, and I assumed the ready position. The first contact was a flying kick to my ribs, which I easily blocked with a downward thrust. I cartwheeled out of the ninja's path, feeling the cap leave my head again and know-ing it didn't matter a damn bit if it did—not anymore. I pressed forward with a two-pointed attack, my arms flying. The ninja blocked me. I was vaguely aware that the pavilion was filling up with people—the police team moving in. They could have been a bunch of schoolkids for all the difference it made to me. If I let my attention waver from the ninja for one second, I was a goner.

Out of the corner of my eye I saw Teddy's crumpled body lying on the cement. "Get up, Teddy!" I shrieked. "Run, run!"

I saw him stir but couldn't wait around to see what he'd do next. Dust rose into the streetlit sky as the ninja pressed me back across the pavilion toward the wall. Block, block—kick, kick. I somersaulted off to the side to keep him (I assumed it was a him) from driving me toward the low wall—beyond it was a steep incline I didn't much feel like exploring. If only I'd had the Whisper of Death.

"Heaven, get out of the way!" I heard Detective Wachter's voice calling to me. But I was too deep in the zone. The ninja and I were close now. I could see his eyes, smell his sweat as he moved in closer. I slipped one fist through his defenses and bashed his windpipe. He back-flipped a few feet away and huffed behind his mask, eyes wild, frozen for a moment.

A shot rang out, and he was flying toward me through the air again. *Stupid,* I thought, *the cops are shooting at him.* I prayed their aim was good. I ducked under the ninja's legs, hurling myself to the pavement to avoid his landing. Pain ripped through my knee as I hit the ground with a crunch, paying for my move, and I rolled over just in time to block a dagger the ninja had drawn from the folds of his black gi. I grabbed his wrists, struggling to keep the blade away from me. I knew the ninja was desperate, or he would never have spent so long in one position—that was the rule. If you didn't hit your mark, you kept moving until you did. Stalling in one place only made it easier for your opponent to defeat you—that wasn't martial arts, it was street fighting.

With a grunt I knocked the dagger out of the ninja's hand, and we scrambled over each other toward it like slap-stick comedians. He reached it first and wheeled around, blocking me back into the same position we'd been in before. I cursed myself for being so sloppy. My upper-arm strength was giving out—I was no match for the ninja in this position. I arched my back, trying to get some leverage to hurl him off me, but I couldn't. I managed to slide up so that he wasn't aiming at my face, but as the dagger came closer to my chest, I smelled the sickening smell of his breath, fishy and damp.

Ka-blam! Another shot rang out and I braced for the impact I was sure was coming. It would be just my luck, I figured. Instead the ninja's eyes widened, and the dagger clattered to the pavement near my head. The ninja slumped on top of me.

"Aaargh," I grunted as I threw the deadweight off me and sat up. I didn't want to do it, but I forced myself to pull the mask off my dead attacker's face. Right before it came free, I wondered briefly if he was the same ninja who'd killed Ohiko but then dismissed the thought—*that* ninja had fought like no one I'd ever seen before—not even Hiro was that smooth. This ninja was hardly a match even for me. Very third rate. Someone's funds seemed to be running out.

He was Japanese. I'd seen that face before. I would have bet my life on it. I tried to memorize his features—this was exactly the key I needed to get some answers. I stared at his gaping, empty eyes and the small sharp nose, willing my memory to deliver its secret.

No go.

Blood trickled from the corner of his mouth. It occurred to me suddenly that it was my fault he was dead—and it felt good. I closed my eyes.

"Heaven! Are you okay?" Detective Wachter came sprinting across the pavilion toward me, Detective Martin right behind him. I forced myself to open my eyes and turned around just as droves of policemen wearing bullet-proof vests emerged from around the building. It was like someone had let loose a herd of wild cops on the place. The detectives reached me and each grabbed one of my arms, pulling me up. "Did he cut you?"

"I'm fine, I'm fine," I said. It was strange—but fighting with the ninja had actually been . . . *fun*. Was I getting totally psychopathic about everything? Or was it just that I'd known I had backup, which made it hard to believe I'd really get hurt? It was a strange feeling all around. The guy was *dead*, and I was acting like I'd just won a game of volleyball or something.

"That was just so freaking awesome," Detective Martin said, a huge grin on her face. "I had no idea you could do that!"

I slapped her outstretched hand. Time enough to think about the ninja's identity later. "Yeah, well, all in a day's work." I wiped the dust off my pants and massaged my knee. "Where's Teddy?" I asked, trying to sound noncha-lant.

Detective Wachter frowned. "Gone. We couldn't move in because we didn't want to risk anything happening to you. We had some guys tailing him out of the parking lot, but they lost him almost immediately—he ditched his car." The detective looked at me thoughtfully. "What spooked him back there?"

I looked into Detective Wachter's blue eyes and knew that he knew I'd tipped Teddy off. "I had this feeling something wasn't right . . . and then the ninja . . . ," I said vaguely.

"So ninjas really do attack you a lot?" Detective Martin asked.

"Seems weird, huh?" I answered.

"A little," she said, chuckling.

"I feel bad about that," I said, gesturing down at my fallen attacker. It seemed like the right thing to say. One of the cops moved in with a sheet and spread it over the body.

"Don't worry," Detective Martin said. "After all, you didn't kill him."

"I guess not," I said doubtfully, starting to feel the familiar weakness that always came over me after the adrenaline of battle stopped pumping. "So you guys see this kind of stuff all the time, huh?"

"Believe me, this is nothing," Detective Martin said.

"Well, we'll get him next time," Detective Wachter interrupted, sighing. "Thanks for trying."

"Sorry about that," I said, trying to sound actually sorry. "You know, Detective," I continued as we walked back toward the police car, my knees trembling a little, "it's not Teddy you should be worrying about—it's his father. Yoji Yukemura is behind all these deals."

"Believe me, we know that," Detective Wachter said,

sliding into the driver's seat. "But there are all sorts of reasons we can't go after Yoji—first of all, we have no jurisdiction over him. He can come to the U.S. and pretty much do whatever he wants—that is, unless we actually *watch* him kill someone. And that would never happen. That's what the yakuza are all about, Heaven, you know that. Just like the mafia here, they're very good at keeping the 'godfather' disconnected from their real dirty work."

"Just wishful thinking, I guess," I murmured as we drove back to the police station. I thought about what I had learned and tried to figure out the big picture. If the guys Teddy had been with in Mexico *were* Yukemura men, then why had the men followed us in the SUV? I was positive I'd seen the face of the Yukemura kidnapper back there. Maybe it was just one more screwup in my long, long list.

"So are you going to go back to Japan now?" Detective Martin asked, craning her neck around to look at me.

I stared out the window at Los Angeles. Night had fallen, but the city was filled with light. I wondered what it would be like to see Tokyo again.

"I don't know," I said. "I guess I'll figure it out tomorrow."

Oh my, Heaven is quite a different girl since the wedding. Quite different. So much more sure of herself, more confident . . . not the daddy's little princess I saw at the wedding. This explains why it's been so difficult to locate her. She's grown from a puppy into a full-grown—well, it's not polite to say.

This suite really is delightful. The linens are the finest, the mattress firm. It's almost enough to make me want to stay in bed for a moment or two more. Just a moment or two. Aaah, yes . . .

"Kord! Bring me a cup of tea."

My servant, Kord, bows from the doorway and goes to get the tea. I'll rise when it arrives. No need to rush just now. Haven't I been working night and day like a dog?

Yes, at the wedding she was useless. Pretty, certainly. In fact, quite exquisite, but overcoddled and dull seeming, with none of that spark of intelligence and fire that a woman needs. After the attack I'd assumed they'd find her a few blocks away, shivering in her kimono, then lead her back to the hotel like a good little lamb, a dutiful little daughter. That was the plan, anyway.

Quite remarkable, when you come to think of it. The girl has managed to elude both the Kogos and the Yukemuras—and whoever else—since she fled. I give her young friend Hiro much of the credit for that. But as they say, "the jig is up." It's time for us to finish this thing for good. We can't have Little Miss Heaven careening across the West Coast of the U.S., leaving a trail of bodies in her path, can we? And that unfortunate incident with the ninja last night, tsk, tsk . . . such a waste.

My poor sister. Mieko told me she wants Heaven home immediately. Mieko is a sensitive woman, refined, and her nerves are absolutely raw from all these false starts, all this waiting, all these plans that have died or been aborted at different phases of their execution. It's really been too much for the poor thing to bear. Of course, she also has to keep up appearances with Konishi, and that's a task no woman should have to suffer. At his bedside every day, accepting visits from those horrible old biddies with their condolences. Oh, it's too much. Just too much.

I must make sure that Kord has properly packed my bags for the flight. I think I'll take breakfast in my room this morning so I can make the necessary arrangements.

I am confident Heaven will return with me.

What other choice does she have?

Ah, my tea.

Masato

14

It was night. The crickets were chirping, and I felt the coolness of the dew beneath my bare feet as I walked across the grass. The air smelled like cherry blossoms, a sweet scent carried by the night breeze. When I first saw the speck of light, it seemed far, far away, and I wondered if it might be a firefly or even a match struck to light a candle or a lantern. But soon the light grew stronger and I saw that it was a flame, and that whoever was carrying the torch was walking toward me.

I felt no fear, so I continued across the broad lawn to meet whoever it was. I was walking on the grounds of my father's Tokyo compound, out behind the guest houses where the thick grass curved down a hill toward a stream that bordered one side of the property. Next to the stream was a thicket of trees, a small wooded area where Ohiko and I had played as children.

It suddenly occurred to me that it was my brother who held the torch, and joy filled me as he approached. I was conscious that this was a dream, one of the vivid, lifelike ones I'd had right after he was killed—but I didn't care. It felt like a real visit from the beyond, and I was happy to speak with my brother again, whether on this plane of existence or some other one.

He stopped about five feet away from me, and before I could go to him, he held the torch up so that the flames blocked his face. I could have easily walked around the torch, but somehow I knew that it was a warning—if I ventured too far, I'd be burned. I wanted so much to see his face.

"Ohiko, put the torch down," I said.

"I can't," he replied, in that voice that was so familiar to me, almost as familiar as my own.

"What should I do?" I asked. "Should I go back to Japan?" The part of me that knew I was dreaming decided that I would do whatever Ohiko told me to. But he was silent. "Ohiko?" I ventured, wanting at least to hear his voice again.

Ohiko turned and walked up the hill, and I followed him, mesmerized by the flickering of the torch. After a moment time shifted, and we were all of a sudden inside the house, walking down the long hallway toward the kitchen. The only light was coming from Ohiko's torch. Being in the familiar hall filled me with comfort, and I somehow knew that everyone was right where they were supposed to be—my father and Mieko, both sleeping in their beds, the servants done with their duties for the night, and our old nanny, Harumi, snoring in her sitting room.

Ohiko turned when he reached the kitchen and continued into the east wing of the house, where our bedrooms had been. When he stepped into my room, he walked over to the window and stopped, the torch still held up to block his face. I looked around, surprised that nothing had changed—there was my futon, made up as if ready for me to jump right into after a long night of studying or watching DVDs with Katie. The maids had straightened the piles of book and CDs, and there weren't any clothes lying on the floor like there would have been if I was home. But it was all there . . . just waiting for me.

"Are you telling me to come home?" I asked Ohiko, and started to cry.

Ohiko lowered his torch, and I caught a brief glimpse of his face. He was crying, too.

Then the torch went out.

I woke up, shaken, and wiped the tears from my face. After Ohiko had died, many of the dreams I'd had were comforting: Ohiko and I were children again, playing by the pool, or else Ohiko was as he'd been the last time I'd seen him in Japan, coming to me with a smile on his face, telling me not to worry. But this dream was different—more real somehow. I felt like I'd actually been with my brother for a second, and now I felt the loss of his death, his absence all over again. I wasn't sure what it meant.

But it was pretty clear I needed to go back to Japan to find out.

I wiped my eyes and hauled myself off the cot and over to the tin sink, where I splashed cold water on myself. In a few minutes, after I'd shaken free of the dream's grip, I felt better rested than I had in weeks.

"Good morning, Heaven." I turned and saw Detective Wachter slide open the bars as he balanced two cups of coffee and a Krispy Kreme bag in one hand. "Time for breakfast," he said with a smile.

"Wow, thanks," I said. "Who told you Krispy Kremes were my favorite?"

"Aren't they everyone's?" he said, handing me the bag and one of the coffees. "I wasn't sure how you like it, so I just got black," he added apologetically.

"Black is good," I said, and tore into a maple doughnut. Man, I loved those things. So sugary and sweet they made your teeth hurt. But the way they melted in your mouth . . . I peeked into the bag. Three more, including a chocolate covered—all my favorites. "Don't you want one?" I asked him.

"No, thanks," he said, sitting down on a folding chair the guard had pushed into the cell. "I've already had twice as many as I should have." He rubbed his stomach gingerly.

Hooray, I thought, *massive doughnut binge for me!* I

was starved, as per usual, so I sat down on the bed and set to work on doughnut number two—French cruller.

"So what have you decided?" Detective Wachter asked, taking a sip of his coffee.

I chewed my doughnut thoughtfully, then took a swig of coffee. "I'm not totally sure yet, to be honest," I said.

"Well, I think I should tell you what happens if you decide to stay here." Detective Wachter leaned forward on the folding chair. He had circles under his eyes, and I felt bad remembering how I'd ruined his sting. I hoped he got a promotion or something anyway. He was nice, and not bad looking for an older guy, either.

"Okay," I agreed, through a mouthful of doughnut.

"If you stay here, we *can* offer you police protection for the time being. But I can't guarantee your safety once you leave the station. We'll do everything in our power, but . . ." He shrugged, searching for words.

"But the yakuza are everywhere," I supplied.

Detective Wachter sighed. "Unfortunately, yes. And their resources are far greater than ours. But even forgetting about that," he continued, "we've checked with the INS, and you only have a couple of months left on your tourist visa. If you accept police custody, we'll have to send you back to Japan at the end of that time. If you don't want our protection—you could probably avoid being deported indefinitely. But—you'll be on your own."

"I see," I said, reaching into the bag for another

doughnut. "So staying here is only a temporary fix, you're saying?"

"Well, it all depends on what you want to achieve while you're here. If two months will do it, then it seems to me you're set."

"What about Hiro?" I asked. I didn't know why I trusted Detective Wachter so much, but ever since I'd met him, I'd know that he was a kind man—and wise. Perception be damned—that was just the good, old-fashioned vibe he gave off. And he seemed as good a person as any to ask for advice. After all—who else could I go to? I knew what Masato would say and even Hiro—Hiro would tell me I was crazy to go back to Japan. But I wasn't ready to deal with that part of the equation yet anyway—not quite.

"He's still in the motel. We've been watching his house for the last two days, and we think it's safe for him to return. He's legal here, you know, so there's no reason for him not to go back home. He'll probably be heading over there later this morning."

I fished a napkin out of the bag and wiped my hands, then stared longingly at the next doughnut—custard filled. "I just can't do it." I sighed.

"Go back to Japan?" Detective Wachter asked, his eyebrows kitting together.

"No—tackle that last doughnut. I might OD on the sugar."

Detective Wachter grinned, and I laughed. It felt good,

after all that had happened and all the decisions that needed to be made, to at least know one thing for sure— there was no way I could eat that last doughnut.

"So what do you think I should do?" I asked. Detective Wachter rubbed his eyes, then looked at me hard.

"I think you know what you need to do," he said, standing. "Your uncle will be here in a few minutes."

As if on cue, the guard appeared at the bars and announced that Masato had arrived.

I followed the detective out into the lobby of the precinct, ignoring the jeers of the other inmates. I was getting to feel downright at home in the L.A. jail. Masato stood at the front desk, looking like he'd smelled a very bad smell but just as immaculately dressed as he'd been the first time I met him—today he wore a gray silk pin-striped suit with a pale blue shirt, complete with silver (platinum?) cuff links. In his hands he held a portfolio of soft, ebony leather. Not the type of guy you'd expect to find at central booking, that was for sure.

"Hello, Uncle," I said, bowing.

"Niece," he replied, trying to smile but looking like he just wanted to get out of the police station as fast as he could. "Hello, Detective." They shook hands. "So," Masato said, turning to me, "the police phoned me this morning with the details of your 'sting,' as they say. Such a shame it didn't work out, but the police tell me they are very grateful for your assistance nonetheless."

Detective Wachter bowed slightly and nodded.

"So have you made your decision?" Masato asked, a note of impatience creeping into his voice.

"Almost," I said. "I just need to make one quick phone call. Is that okay?"

Masato looked at his watch. "We need to leave here in under fifteen minutes if we're going to catch our flight. I like to be early for these things. One never knows what will happen these days, does one?" he said, looking at Detective Wachter as if for confirmation.

"Traffic can get pretty bad around here," Detective Wachter agreed, smiling a little bit. I wondered what he thought of Masato and his fancy clothes, his slightly prissy ways. The detective looked like he'd been wearing the same khaki-colored suit his whole life. But I guess you didn't get to be a detective without being able to handle all types of people.

"I'll be just one second," I said to Masato. "I promise." I turned to Detective Wachter. "I need . . ."

"The motel number?" Detective Wachter guessed, fishing around in his pocket. "Hiro asked me to give you this when I spoke with him last night."

"Thanks," I said, and took the scrap of paper down the hall to the pay phone, leaving my uncle and the detective to engage in no doubt awkward conversation.

"Hello?"

I caught my breath as Hiro's sleepy voice came on the

line. Over the last few days I'd pushed all thoughts of him out of my mind, trying so hard to simply focus on the situation at hand. I thought about what had happened in the hotel room in Tijuana and how it seemed so impossibly long ago that Hiro had first admitted he had feelings for me—and that I'd admitted the same thing to him.

"Hello? Heaven, is that you?"

"Just tell me one thing," I said, before he could ask me anything about what I'd been doing for the last few days. "When we were in Yoji's suite and he told you that if you worked for him, you could see your father again and live like a king and defend your family's honor . . . were you tempted? At all?"

I waited for Hiro's answer. It all depended on what he said—it could go either way. For me, this was the root of the matter. I could hear him breathing on the other end of the line, and my heart raced faster and faster as the silence went on and on. And then, just when I thought I couldn't stand it anymore—

"Yes," he said, his voice defeated and lost. My first instinct was to argue with him, to make him take it back, but I knew, deep down, that he was telling the truth. I felt like I'd been hit in the belly with a bo stick—worse, really. That kind of pain wore off after a minute or so, but I knew that this kind of hurt would never go away.

"Good-bye, Hiro," I said, and hung up the phone. I leaned my head against the wall. Hiro and I were more alike

SAMURAI GIRL

than I'd ever imagined. We knew we shouldn't want the things that crime had supplied us with our whole lives, yet a small part of us still wanted them. I was convinced that if we stayed together in L.A., if we stayed together at *all*, that eventually we'd talk each other into some kind of complacency. It would just be so much *easier* to give in to it together. How could we be warriors when what we really wanted was a life together? There was no room for that in the bushido. And even though Hiro seemed to think it would be okay to bend some of the rules, I wasn't so sure about that myself. Besides, it was time for me to follow my own path. My family needed me, and my duty was to them.

I took a deep breath and walked down the hallway to where my uncle waited.

"All right," I said. "Take me home."

202